Byomkesh Bakshi

Byomkesh Bakshi

Stories by
Saradindu Bandopadhyay

Translated by
Monimala Dhar

RUPA

Published by
Rupa Publications India Pvt. Ltd.
7/16, Ansari Road, Daryaganj,
New Delhi 110 002

Sales Centres:

Allahabad Bengaluru Chennai
Hyderabad Jaipur Kathmandu
Kolkata Mumbai

Typeset in 11 pts. Palermo by
Mindways Design
1410 Chiranjiv Tower
43 Nehru Place
New Delhi 110 019

Printed in India by
B.B. Press
A-37, Sector-67
Noida 201 301

Contents

Acknowledgements

I would like to convey my gratitude to my husband, Prof. P.P. Dhar, for his constant support and patient, hard work in typing out a few stories, in spite of his busy schedule; my daughter, Amrita, whose idea it was that I should translate Byomkesh stories into English; Paromita Das who helped to type many of the stories and last but not the least, Rupa and Co. without whose encouragement it would have been impossible to get the stories published.

Monimala Dhar

An Introduction

Saradindu Bandopadhyay was born on the 30th of March, 1899, in Purnea, Bihar, where his father was posted. His original home was in Baranagar, near Calcutta. After completing his graduation in 1919, he passed his law examination in 1926. But he left the legal profession and became a full-fledged writer from the year 1929. He was called to the Mumbai film world as a script writer. In 1941, he left Mumbai and settled permanently in Pune where he breathed his last in the early 70s.

His writings were immensely popular during the 60s and 70s. He has written a large number of novels, novellas, long and short stories, historical fiction and reincarnation stories, plays, belles-lettres — and last but not the least — detective stories and novels featuring Byomkesh Bakshi — The Truth Seeker or *Satyanneshi*, who hated to be called a detective! These stories were written within the vast span of 1932 to 1970. There are over thirty five Byomkesh thrillers in the form of long and short stories, novels and novellas.

Byomkesh was introduced in the story — *Satyanneshi* where he first meets Ajit Bandopadhyay in a mess-house, while staying there incognito, to solve a case. Ajit, the writer, then joins Byomkesh and becomes his constant companion, even after Byomkesh marries and settles down.

Byomkesh Bakshi was popularised by Doordarshan in a serial with the same name featuring the well-known actor Rajit Kapoor. Satyajit Ray also picturised a novella by Saradindu — "Chiriakhana" or "The Zoo". I hope the readers find the stories enthralling and interesting as I found them when I read them in the original.

Monimala Dhar

The Deadly Diamond
(Raktamukhi Neela)

Byomkesh had put up his legs on a table and was fidgeting his feet restlessly. The newspaper was open on his lap. On this monsoon morning, we were spending an idle day at home. The last four days had been spent similarly. We were feeling depressed about spending this day in the same way. The constant movement of his feet, did not disturb his concentration. He was reading the paper. I was smoking a cigarette — none of us was exchanging any words. But how long could we keep quiet? Just for the sake of talking, I said, "Is there any news?"

Byomkesh spoke without lifting his eyes from the paper, "The news is serious. Two culprits have been released."

Hopefully, I said, "Who are they?"

"One is Saratchandra's *Charitraheen* — he has been released in some cinema halls. The other is Ramanath Neogi — he was released from the Alipur jails. It is a ten day old news — and Kalketu has kindly published it only today!" He turned the paper in frustration and got up.

I realised that he had lost patience because of this dearth of news. It was unfair that on such a rainy day there was no crunchy and hot news. I asked, "Who is Ramanath Neogi?"

Byomkesh began pacing the room. He looked out of the window towards a dull and wet day and said, "Neogi is not an unknown person — a few years back his name was published in large print on newspaper."

"You have not answered my question — who is he?"

"He is a thief — not a petty pilferer but a jewel thief. He was as intelligent as bold and daring," Byomkesh heaved a sigh of regret, " Nowadays one doesn't find such great criminals."

I said sarcastically, "It is really the misfortune of our country. But why was his name printed in large letters?"

"Because at last he was caught and tried in a court of law." Byomkesh picked up a cigarette from a tin and lit it carefully, relaxed in his chair and said, "I still remember the incidents although it was ten years ago. I had just started my work — it was long before I met you."

I noticed that though he had started talking casually, he was gradually becoming animated as he recalled the past. I thought that it was better to listen to an interesting story on a dull, lazy, rainy day, rather than be bored. So I said, "Tell me the story."

Byomkesh said, "There is no story — but the whole incident is a mystery to me. The police had worked very hard and showed some success too but could not retrieve the real thing."

"What was the real thing?"

"During that year, there was a sudden spate of jewellry theft in this city of Calcutta — today Jawaharlal Hiralal was robbed, the next day Dutta jewellers was burgled — in fifteen days at least five large shops suffered great losses, mounting to lakhs of rupees. Police started investigating.

"Then, there was a burglary in Maharaja Ramendra Sinha's house. I won't insult your knowledge by telling you who he is. There are very few Bengalis who are not acquainted with his name. He is as rich as he is benevolent. There are few like him nowadays. He is in a bit of trouble now — but let that be. He was a collector of precious stones. The stones were displayed in a glass case in a room in the second floor of his house. The room was guarded continuously — and very well. But even then there was a break in. Two guards were found lying unconscious and quite a few jewels were stolen.

"Maharaja had a blue diamond in his collection — he treasured this stone because he thought that it brought him luck — he wore it in a ring. But lately the stone had become loose. So he had kept it in the room and was thinking of calling a jeweller to reset it in another ring. This blue diamond was also stolen.

"I don't know how much knowledge you have of diamonds. But blue diamonds are rare and exquisite stones. The value of blue diamonds doesn't depend only on their weight but are priced, especially in our country, on their powers of changing the fortune of a person. The blue diamond is supposed to be the stone of the planet Saturn. It is common belief that if a blue diamond is worn and it suits the person — he can rise from rags to riches and if it does not suit a person, he can become a pauper. The effect of the blue diamond is either very good or very bad depending on the person wearing it, and whether it suits the person. So the value of these blue diamonds is not determined by their weight. I have seen a Marwari gentleman paying thousands for a tiny piece of blue diamond. I am not superstitious by nature but even I have been forced to admit the powers of this particular stone.

"Anyway, when this diamond was stolen from his house — the Maharaja raised a great hue and cry. Although he had lost thousands of rupees worth of precious stones he was most concerned about this particular diamond. He announced that even if the thief was not caught, and if anyone could give him back the diamond he would reward him amply. The police started investigating with great gusto — they even employed their detective Nirmal babu for the job.

"Nirmal babu is unknown to you, but he is really very intelligent. I was fortunate to know him, he has retired now. Within seven days, Nirmal babu recovered all the stolen jewels with the burglar — who was no other than our Ramanath Neogi. Although all the stones were found after searching his house, the blue diamond was missing.

"Later, Ramanath was consigned to the jail for twelve years after a long court case. But still the diamond was not found. Ramanath refused to speak. But Maharaja Ramendra Sinha began pressurising the police to retrieve his diamond. So much so, that after three months of imprisonment, Ramanath's cell was searched by no other than Nirmal babu. Police spies in the guise of prisoners, had informed that they had seen the stone on Ramanath. But nothing was found. Ramanath was in Alipur jail at that time — but where he had hidden the diamond in that small cell, was a real mystery.

The police gradually gave up the search."

Byomkesh was silent for a few minutes, then spoke to himself, "Strange problem — where could a prisoner hide a stone as big as a cardamom pea. If I was investigating the case, I may have found it and could have won the reward,"

In the middle of Byomkesh's soliloquy we heard footsteps on the stairs outside. I sat up, "That must be a client, Byomkesh." Byomkesh listened attentively and said, "Old man, costly shoes, they can be heard even on this rainy day. Probably roams around in cars — so he is wealthy. He limps a little….." Suddenly in an excited voice, Byomkesh said, "Ajit, look out of the window and see if a huge Rolls Royce is standing at our door — yes? Then I am right. What co-incidence, Ajit, the person we were speaking of, Maharaja Ramendra Sinha has come to me — do you know why?"

I said excitedly, "I know, I saw the news in the paper. His secretary Haripada Rakshit has been murdered recently — maybe that's why…."

There was a knock at the door. Byomkesh welcomed the visitor warmly and reverentially. Although I had often seen his photographs in newspapers — this was the first time I had seen him in person. There was no pomp or grandeur surrounding him. He seemed a simple, frail person. There was some problem in his leg for which he limped a little. He was over sixty but his skin was not wrinkled — he had an air of calm dignity.

Maharaja smiled questioningly at Byomkesh, he was a little surprised too, "It seems from your expression that you were waiting for me. Did you guess that I was going to visit you?"

Byomkesh too smiled, "I can't believe my good fortune. But when the police could not solve the murder of your secretary, I hoped that you might ask for my help. But first, please take your seat."

The Maharaja sat on a chair and said slowly, "Yes, five or six days have already passed. The police have been able to do nothing. So I thought I would pay you a visit, hoping that you might be able to help. I had gradually become very fond of Haripada — besides the way he died was terrible."

The Maharaja stopped awhile, "Of course, he was not a saint. But you must be knowing that it is a fancy of mine to bring wayward people on the right path. If you consider him from all angles — Haripada was not a bad person. He was very good at his work. Moreover his heart was full of gratitude for me — I had received proof of that too."

Byomkesh said, "Excuse me, I was not aware that Haripada was not a good man. What evil deed was he involved in?"

The Maharaja said, "According to the man on the street, he was a hardened criminal. He had been sent to jail several times. The last time he came out of prison, he met me."

Byomkesh said, "Please start from the very beginning. I have read the news in the papers but it is so inadequate that I could not come to any conclusion. Please assume that I know nothing and relate every detail — that will help me to understand the case."

The Maharaja said, "All right, I will do that." Then clearing his throat, he began, "It was about six months back — about the middle of February that Haripada first came to see me. He had come out of the jail the previous day, he disclosed everything to me and concealed nothing. He told me that if I gave him a chance to live an honest life he would never go back to his criminal ways.

"I felt sorry for him. He was below forty but already he had visited the jail four times. The last time he had been caught on charges of theft and forgery. His sentence was a long one. I found that he was sincerely repentant. I asked him what he could do. He said that he did not have much chance to study because he had been sent to jail several times after the age of nineteen. Even then he had managed to learn shorthand and typing. He assured me that if I employed him, he would serve me faithfully.

"My heart softened towards Haripada, the very first time that I saw him. For some reason I cannot ignore the appeal of this type of people. So, although I did not need a shorthand typist, I employed him. He rented a small house nearby, as he had no relatives.

"Soon I noticed that the man was very efficient and intelligent. He did things which he was not supposed to do, very perfectly. He did a lot of my work in advance. Within two months, his services became indispensable to me — I couldn't do without him.

"Just at that time, my old secretary Abinash babu died. I appointed Haripada in his place. My employees were not happy about this appointment — but I did not bother. I knew that Haripada was the most suitable man for the job.

"For the last four months Haripada had dispensed his duties of a secretary very efficiently. Other employees complained about him, but I ignored them. It is true that Haripada was a jailbird but I can assure you that at the end he was a changed person. I think that poverty had turned him into a criminal and as soon as he overcame that problem, he turned over a new leaf. In fact we should try to reform criminals who have gone to the jails for similar reasons.

"Anyway, what happened last Tuesday was unthinkable. You must have read about the incident in the newspapers. I got the news in the morning that Haripada was murdered. I informed the police and went to his house myself. He was lying on the floor of his bedroom — the whole room was bespattered with blood. The murderer had cut his throat so mercilessly that even now I shiver to think of it. His windpipe was torn to shreds. You could not have seen a murder committed with such bestial violence."

Maharaja stopped for some time and shivered when he tried to recall that moment.

Byomkesh asked, "Was there no other wound on his body?"

The Maharaja said, "Yes, he was stabbed to death. The doctor said that his throat was cut after he was stabbed. So the murderer must have stabbed him fatally and then cut his throat. How cruel it was! I can't imagine how human beings behave like senseless animals."

Everyone was quiet for sometime. The Maharaja was probably thinking of animals called human beings. Byomkesh was deep in thought, too.

Suddenly I noticed Byomkesh's half-closed eyes. I became excited at once. That same expression — I had seen it often — there was no mistake! Byomkesh had found a clue.

The Maharaja broke his silence and said, "I have told you whatever I know. I want you to work together with the police to solve this case. I feel that this cruel murderer should not be allowed to roam freely in society — it is everyone's moral duty to catch him. I hope you don't mind taking up this case."

Byomkesh said, "I have no quarrel with the police — we will surely work together. Can you tell me the duration of Haripada's last term in jail?"

Maharaja said, "Haripada had told me that his last term was of fourteen years but because of his good behaviour, he was released after eleven years."

Byomkesh said happily, "Can you tell me anything else about Haripada?"

Maharaja said, "What exactly do you want to know?"

Byomkesh said, "Did you notice anything unnatural in his behaviour a few days before his death?"

The Maharaja said, "Yes, three or four days before his death, Haripada was doing his work near me one morning, when he became very ill. Looking at him I felt that he was terrified for some reason."

"Was there no one near you at that time?"

The Maharaj thought for some time and said, "I was going through the applications of some people who were asking for alms. One petitioner was present there."

"Haripada took ill in front of that man — did he?"

"Yes."

After a minute of silence Byomkesh asked, "Can you think of anything else?"

Maharaja thought for some time and said, "I remembered a small incident. I don't know if you remember that a few years back a blue diamond had been stolen from my house."

"Yes, I do remember."

"You must be knowing then that I had announced a reward for its return."

"I know that too, but I don't know if the reward still stands."

The Maharaja said, "This is the question Haripada asked me when he first took the job of a typist. I was surprised because I had given up all hope of even getting back the diamond."

"What answer did you give to Haripada?"

"I said that I will certainly give the reward if I get back the blue diamond."

Byomkesh sprang up, "If I ask you the same question — will your answer be the same too?"

The Maharaja looked surprised, "Yes, of course — but—"

Byomkesh sat down again, — "Do you want to know the name of Haripada's murderer?"

The Maharaja was stunned, he said, "I can't understand anything. Do you know the name of Haripada's murderer?"

"I know the name but it is not my job to gather evidence against him — that is the job of the police. I will only tell you his name — then the police can search his house and find the proof. I don't think that will be difficult."

"This seems like magic, do you really know the name of the culprit?" the Maharaja asked, overwhelmed.

"Right now I am just assuming — but I know that my assumption will not be wrong — the name of the murderer is Ramanath Neogi."

"Ramanath Neogi? — the name sounds familiar."

"Of course it will sound familiar. Ten years back, he had stolen your diamond — he has just come out of jail."

"Yes, I remember, but why did he kill Haripada? — What was the relation between the two?"

"There is a relation between them — if I go through old documents in the prison, it will become clear. But it is now nearly eleven, I won't detain you here any more. If you please come back here at four in the afternoon, everything will become clear to you. May be you will also get back your diamond — I will see to everything."

After bidding good-bye to the stunned Maharaja — Byomkesh started getting ready to go out.

I asked, "Where are you going out so late in the day?"

He said, "I will have to go through some old papers in the jail office. Besides I have other things to do. I don't know when I will return. If I get time I will have lunch in some hotel." Saying this, he went out with his raincoat and umbrella in the pouring rain.

He returned at about three in the afternoon. While opening his shoes he said, "I am very hungry — I haven't eaten anything. I will have a quick bath. Putiram, please prepare something for me. At four, the matinee show will begin."

Surprised, I said, "What show? Where?"

Byomkesh said, "Don't worry. The show will be held here in this room. Ajit, please place a few more chairs for the spectators." He went in to bathe.

While he was eating, I asked, "What did you do the whole day long?"

Byomkesh put a large chunk of omlette in his mouth. Chewing with great relish, he said, "I have a friend in the jail department, I went to him first. There I went through the old records and found that my assumption is correct."

"What was your assumption?"

Byomkesh ignored my question and continued speaking, "After finishing my work there I went to Buddhu babu — sorry — Bidhu babu the police inspector. The area in which Haripada was murdered falls under his jurisdiction. The police officer in-charge of the murder is Purna babu. I explained everything to Purna babu. Then I buttered Bidhu babu sufficiently to get my work done."

"But, what work?" I asked desperately.

"The work is to find Ramanath Neogi's present address, secondly, to arrest him and search his house. It was easy to find his address but the search was fruitless. The only thing discovered in his room was a huge, sharp knife. It has been sent for forensic test to find traces of human blood. But what I hoped to find was not there. The man's gift for concealing things is just amazing."

"What thing?"

"The Maharaja's diamond."

"Now what will you do?"

"Some acting. I will strike at the root of the superstitious fear in Ramanath — lets see if I get any result. There! The Maharaja has arrived. The others will soon arrive too."

"Who are the others?"

"Ramanath and his custodians."

"They will come here?"

"Yes, that's the arrangement I made with Bidhu babu. Putiram, remove these dishes."

I did not get a chance to ask any more questions. The Maharaja entered the room as the clock struck four. He was punctual, just as expected from a person of his stature.

As soon as he sat down we heard the footsteps of others. Soon, Bidhu babu, Purna babu, two sub-inspectors and Ramanath entered the room.

There was nothing unusual about Ramanath. Probably his non-descript appearance was a good foil for his profession. He had closely cropped hair, a narrow forehead, a sharp chin and shifty eyes. He wore a very old multi-coloured, leather buttoned sporting coat (made probably before he went to the jail). He wore a pair of unexpectedly large rubber boots. He looked a comic sight. Never would one imagine that he was a dangerous man.

Byomkesh pointed towards Ramanath and asked the Maharaja, "Do you recognize him?"

"Yes, he was the one who came for alms, that day."

"Now, all of you please take your seats. Bidhu babu, you know the Maharaja — please sit next to him. Ramanath, please sit here." Byomkesh pointed to a chair next to the table. Ramanath sat down without a word. The two sub-inspectors sat by his sides. Bidhu babu glared at everything with a superior air of gravity. He could not accept the fact that something unofficial was about to happen in his presence. His expression and behaviour showed that he was very uneasy and indignant about the whole thing.

Byomkesh sat in front of the table when everyone was seated. He began, "I will tell you a story today. It is not an imaginary story like the ones that Ajit writes, but a true story. I will relate it as truthfully and correctly as possible. If I make a mistake Ramanath will correct me. Another person knew this story besides Ramanath — but he is dead."

After this introduction, Byomkesh began his story. Ramanath's face was expressionless. He neither looked up or spoke. He kept on scribbling on the table with his fingers.

"I will begin my story after Ramanath was sent to the jail. Though he was sent to the jail, he did not part with the Maharaja's diamond. How he did this is unknown to me and is not important to my story. Ramanath can disclose it, if he wishes." Ramanath glanced for a second at Byomkesh and continued moving his fingers on the table, with an inscrutable expression. Byomkesh said, "Ramanath had stolen many other precious stones — which were retrieved by the police, with the exception of the blue diamond. He always kept it with him. In all possibility, the stone has a magnetic power, besides it was beautiful to look at — a blue diamond with a red streak in the center. He couldn't resist keeping the stone with him. He also thought that the stone was lucky. But he did not know that it could prove unlucky for some. When misfortune follows a man — he is often misguided by it.

"Anyway, Ramanath was kept in the Alipur jail. After some time the police got to know that the diamond was with him. His cell was searched. He had another companion in the same cell — that man was also searched — but nothing was found. Where was it?

"The second prisoner in the cell was Haripada Rakshit. Haripada was an old criminal. He had spent years in jail right from his childhood. He knew many tricks. Those who deal with jailbirds, know that many criminals can make a kind of pocket inside their throats. It sounds strange but it is a fact. The prisoners cannot take money into the jail. But most of them are addicts of some sort, they need to bribe the wardens to bring drugs from outside. So they keep the money in these bags inside their throats. Those who have served jail terms from an early age, are experts in this. Senior police officers are aware of this.

"Haripada had made a pocket inside his throat. When Ramanath began sharing his cell — the two became quite friendly. He got to know about Haripada's special trick.

"Then the police raided the jail one day. There was no place to hide the diamond. Ramanath, you gave the diamond to Haripada and asked him to hide it in his throat. Haripada was very attracted by the stone — so he swallowed it quickly. The diamond remained inside his throat. No wonder, the police found nothing.

"The very next day, Haripada was transferred to another jail, according to the prison records. Haripada thought himself to be fortunate. He betrayed his friend — he did not return the diamond to Ramanath. Ramanath could not complain to anyone. A thief cannot cry for goods stolen from him. It was from then that Ramanath planned his revenge on Haripada."

I noticed at this point that although there was no change of expression in Ramanath's face, nerves in his forehead were throbbing and his eyes were red. Byomkesh continued,

"Then ten years passed by. Haripada was released from jail. He came straight away to the Maharaja after his release. His intention was to get acquainted with the Maharaja and return the diamond for a reward. He knew that if he tried to sell the diamond outside, he might get caught.

"But the Maharaja was so kind to him right from the beginning that he was in a dilemma. Even then he brought up the subject of the diamond with the Maharaja. But later he felt ashamed to produce the diamond and take the reward from a person who had been so good to him. It is remarkable how the Maharaja's kindness infused a sense of gratitude in the mind of a hardened criminal.

"But Haripada's days were numbered. A few days earlier Ramanath was released from jail. He did not know where Haripada was but as fate would have it, within four days of his release he saw him in the Maharaja's house. It was after seeing Ramanath that Haripada became ill, there was no other reason why he should suddenly become so sick."

"The spark of revenge which was burning in Ramanath's heart for the last ten years burst into flames. It was easy for him to find out where Haripada lived. Then that fateful night, he went there ….."

Till now Byomkesh was facing all of us — now suddenly he turned on Ramanath. Ramanath was staring at Byomkesh with unblinking eyes, like that of a snake. Byomkesh pointed at him with his finger and said in an intense, low, magnetic voice, "Ramanath, that night you tore apart Haripada's throat in search of the diamond, where is it now?"

Ramanath could not look away from Byomkesh's hypnotic gaze. He moistened his lips with the tip of his tongue, tried to stand up and then with great effort tried to break away from Byomkesh's magnetic control. He said in a cracked voice, "I don't know, I don't know. I don't know Haripada. I have not murdered him. I don't know anything about a diamond. It is not with me." He looked at Byomkesh with red, rebellious eyes and held his arms tight across his chest.

Byomkesh's finger was still pointing at him. I felt that we were witnessing the climax of an intense and exciting drama. Two tremendous will powers were fighting a dual. We were waiting in stunned silence to see who would win the last round.

Byomkesh's voice took on a terrible, foreboding note. He bent close to Ramanath and spoke in the same low, intense voice, "Ramanath, you don't realize the curse of this diamond, that is why you are not able to give it up. Just think, till the time you had not stolen this diamond, no one was able to catch you. As soon as you stole it, you were caught and sent to the jail. Then think of what happened to Haripada. He had hidden the diamond in his throat. Look what happened to his throat — no one knows it better than you. If you want to live, give back that terrible diamond. It is not a diamond but poison from cobra. If you wear the diamond in your hand then your hand will be chained. If you wear it in your neck, you will be hanged. That diamond will make you hang in the gallows."

Ramanath stood up with an indistinct sound. We did not realize the terrible storm that was brewing in his heart. He looked around like a madman then tore a button from his coat and threw it away. He screamed with terror, "I don't want it, I don't want it! Take away your cursed diamond — let me live." Saying this he heaved a great sigh and fell into a swoon.

Byomkesh wiped the sweat from his brow. I saw that his hands were trembling. He had won in the fight of wills — but it had taken a toll on him, too.

He picked up the button thrown away by Ramanath — tore away the leather covering and said in a trembling voice, "Maharaja, here is your diamond."

The Hidden Heirloom
(Seemanta Heera)

Byomkesh was out of work for some time now. The people of this country have a bad habit of not even informing the police about small crimes like theft — better to have peace than prosperity — that is their philosophy. If something serious happens — the police get to know but no one spends hard-earned money on a private detective. For some days they moan and groan and complain, even abuse the police, then they forget about the whole thing.

Murders are also committed in our country. But most of the time they are acts of anger — unplanned and unintelligent — so that the murderers are caught at once — put into the jail and later hanged.

So it is not surprising that the Truth Seeker Byomkesh Bakshi had hardly any truth to seek. Byomkesh was not at all bothered about this. He continued reading the newspaper from its north-west corner to the south-east corner in detail and the rest of the time he spent in his library behind closed doors. But I was getting impatient with so much of free time. Though my job was not to catch criminals but to entertain readers with my stories free of cost, in fact that was the motto of my life, I was addicted to the catching of the criminals. As a result, life was getting as boring as a salt-less diet.

So that morning, while drinking tea, I asked Byomkesh, "What has happened, brother? Have the thieves and criminals of Bengal become saints and sages?"

Byomkesh smiled and said, "No, you are getting proof of that in the newspaper everyday."

"True, but why are we not getting a chance to catch them?"

"Patience, we will get a chance. The fish will take the bait at its own time — we can't force it. An intelligent criminal is becoming a paradox in our country — it's not my fault. Most of the names in the police diaries are of small fries. Those big fish hardly swim up to get caught in the net. I am interested in these.

You must be knowing that those ponds or rivers which have large fish are a temptation to people like me."

I said, "Your similes have a fishy stink in them. If there was a psychiatrist here he would have certainly concluded that you would leave your job of truth-seeking and start selling fish."

Byomkesh said, "In that case the psychiatrist would have made a terrible mistake."

Just then there was a knock on the door — the postman delivered a letter. Letters were a rare commodity in our lives — so its arrival instantly aroused our interest. It was an insured letter in Byomkesh's name.

When he pulled out the letter from the envelope, we were more impressed. There was a bronze and blue monogram on top of it. The paper was thick, smooth and expensive, attached to the letter was a cheque of five thousand rupees. Byomkesh read the short letter and passed it to me smilingly, "Take it, a very serious matter. A mystery in the home of a rich elite in North Bengal. I have been asked to go there post-haste — even the traveling expense has been advanced. The secretary of the gentleman has written,

"Kumar Tridib Narayan Roy has asked me to write this letter to you. He has heard about you and wants your help and advice regarding a very serious matter. So we will be grateful if you can come here as soon as possible — let us know which train you are boarding and we will send our car to the station.

Yours etc."

No fact could be gathered from the letter. I said, "It seems very serious. Could you make out anything from the writing or the paper — you are knowledgeable about these things."

"No. But from what I know about the rich in our country, I wouldn't be surprised if Kumar Tridibendra had a nightmare that his pet elephant had been stolen by his rival — frightened, he has called for a detective."

"No, no, I think you are exaggerating. Can't you see that he has already sent so much of money — something serious must have happened."

"That is your mistake. If the patient is wealthy, you think that his illness is also serious. It is usually the opposite. A doctor is called for in case of the rich even to treat a small pimple but a poor dies unattended even if he is seriously ill."

"Anyway, are you going?"

Byomkesh thought for a moment.

"Since I have nothing else to do, let us go for two days. At least we will see some new places — I don't think that you have been to those parts."

I was very eager to go but I hesitated, "Should I go? They have called you only."

Byomkesh smiled, "Nothing is wrong in your going. In fact Kumar Bahadur will be happy to see two of us instead of one. Besides, since someone else is spending the money, it is our moral duty to go. According to the scriptures — we should always go on a pilgrimage at other peoples' expense."

I could not remember which scripture had given such wise advice — anyway I did not need much persuasion to accompany Byomkesh.

We left that evening by train. Nothing much happened in the journey except that we met a very friendly man. There were only three of us in the compartment. After chatting with us for some time, the gentleman asked, "Where are you going?"

In reply, Byomkesh smiled pleasantly and asked, "Where are *you* going?"

The gentleman was a bit bewildered by the question, "I will get down at the next station."

Byomkesh again smiled and said, "We will get down at the station after the next."

There was no need to tell such a lie — but I realised that Byomkesh must be having some reason for doing so. As soon as the train stopped, the gentleman got down. It was dark outside and he soon vanished in the crowd.

After a few stations, I got down at the platform to stretch my legs, when I spotted the gentleman in the compartment next to ours — he was staring at me but as soon as our eyes met, he ducked. Excitedly, I told Byomkesh, "Listen..........."

He said, "I know, the gentleman is in the next compartment. Things are not so simple as they seem. That's good."

After this incident, I tried to trace the gentleman at each station but failed.

Early next morning, we reached our destination. We would have to travel for about six or seven miles by car to reach the house. The station was small, an employee of Mr. Roy was waiting for us with an expensive car. He welcomed us warmly and soon we were on our way — moving fast through the lonely roads.

The employee was elderly and very discreet — because when Byomkesh tried to probe he said that he knew nothing. He was only obeying orders by receiving and taking us to his employer.

We looked at each other and remained quiet for the rest of the journey. When we reached there, we found that we were entering a huge ancient mansion. It consisted of five wings. There was a beautiful garden, hot house, swimming pool, tennis court, guest house etc. There were a lot of workers, servants and employees around. We were taken in by Mr. Roy's private secretary. We were given a whole suite to ourselves. The secretary told us, "Please freshen up and have some refreshments — Kumar Bahadur will also be ready by then to meet you."

After a good breakfast, we were relaxing while smoking, when the secretary came and told us to follow him, Kumar Bahadur was waiting for us in the library. We felt as if we were going to have an audience with a king. The grand welcome, the very name Kumar Tridibendra Narayan Roy — inspired some kind of awe. But when we met him, we found that he was a simply clad, pleasant, fair and good-looking young man — there was no pomposity n his behaviour. He stood up when he saw us, folded his hands in greeting, looked hesitatingly at Byomkesh and said, "Are you Byomkesh babu ?"

Byomkesh introduced me and said, "He is my friend, assistant and future biographer. That's why I always take him along with me wherever I go."

Tridibendra Narayan smiled and said, "I hope your biography won't be written in a long time. I am glad that Ajitbabu has accompanied you. It is through his writings that I got to know about you."

I was filled with joy — the kind, that every writer feels when his writing is mentioned. We realised that although he was wealthy, he was educated and intelligent. The library was packed with different kinds of books. On the table too some books were scattered proving the fact that the library was not only a showpiece but also that the books were regularly used. After some small talk, Kumar Bahadur asked his secretary to leave us alone and also to shut the door behind him.

Then he started speaking, "The job for which I have given you all the trouble and brought you here is very serious and very confidential. So before I tell you anything you have to promise that no other person will know about this matter because it concerns the prestige of our family."

Byomkesh said, "I don't think it is necessary for us to promise anything because we consider all the affairs of our clients as highly confidential — that is our professional etiquette. Anyway, how do you want us to take our vow of secrecy?"

Kumar smiled and said, "There is no need for a vow — your word is equally valuable."

I was a bit hesitant, "Can I not even mention the affair in the form of a story."

A determined Tridib said, "No, I don't want any discussion about this."

I sighed with disappointment at missing a chance of writing a good story. Byomkesh said, "Don't worry, we will not reveal anything."

Kumar was quiet for some time and then said, "We have very old and expensive jewels, stones and diamonds in our family — I don't think you know about it."

Byomkesh said, "I do know a little about those — especially a particular diamond which is rare and exquisite."

"You know about it? Then you must also be knowing that last month there was an exhibition of precious stones in Calcutta — that diamond was shown there."

Byomkesh nodded his head, "Yes, I heard about it but I was not fortunate enough to see the diamond."

Kumar was silent for sometime, "You may never get a chance to see it. It has been stolen."

Byomkesh echoed, "Stolen!"

Tridib said, "That is why I brought you here. Let me start at the very beginning. Our family dates back to the times of the Moghuls. It was during this time that my ancestors were given this land as a gift. My ancestor was a bold and courageous man who persuaded the Emperor to give a deed of grant for the land. We still have that deed with us in the family. The diamond has been handed down from those early days till now. There is a saying that no harm will come to our family if the diamond remains with us but if it goes to any other branch of the family — our family will be destroyed.

The heir to the property is the eldest son — this is the rule of our family. The younger sons will get an allowance. So after my father's death two years ago, I inherited the property. I am an only child. At present, I have an uncle, who gets a few thousands a month as an allowance from the family coffer.

This is just an introduction. Now let me tell you how the diamond disappeared. When I got the invitation to exhibit my diamond in the Exhibition — I took it in a special train to Calcutta. I only heaved a sigh of relief when I handed it over to the organisers. You must be knowing that in this exhibition exquisite jewels and diamonds from the royal families of Baroda, Hyderabad, Patiala etc. were displayed — it was a prestigious affair and the Government itself was responsible. So it seemed impossible for the diamond to get stolen. It was kept in a glass case and only I had the keys to it.

The exhibition went on for seven days. On the eighth day I came back home with the diamond. It was then that it was discovered that it had been stolen and what I had brought home was only an inexpensive imitation worth about two hundred rupees."

Kumar was silent. Byomkesh asked, "Didn't you let the police or the organisers know about the theft?"

Kumar said, "That would have been useless, because as soon as the theft was discovered, I knew who had stolen the diamond."

"Oh!" said Byomkesh and looked searchingly at Kumar, "Please continue."

Kumar said, "It is not a matter to be discussed. I did not even let my close family know about it in case there was a scandal and people got to know about it or if it went to the press. The only other person who knows about it is our old Dewan who looks after the finances of our family."

"I will tell you everything in detail. I have already told you that I have an uncle. He stays in Calcutta and gets few thousands as an allowance from the estate. You must have heard about him. He is a famous artist and a scientist, Sir Digindra Narayan Roy. He is a strange man. If he was born abroad, he would have been recognised as a genius. His knowledge is vast and he is extremely intelligent. In his young days he had discovered some unknown facts about the plaster of paris — he was knighted by the British Government. Even in the world of arts, his talents are well-known — you must have heard about him. Everyone knows about the accolades he won in an art exhibition in Paris where he exhibited a stone statue of Lord Shiva, sculpted by him. A multi-faceted person like him is a rare phenomenon." Kumar smiled.

"My uncle has a great deal of affection for me but we don't agree about one thing. He asked me for that diamond. He had an unnecessary desire for it. It was not for its monetary value that he wanted it — he just wished desperately to possess it."

I asked, "How expensive is the diamond?"

"Probably, three crores or more. No one can buy it with money in our country. Besides, we never evaluated it. It was regarded as an auspicious charm in our family — it was priceless.

Anyway, my uncle even asked my father for the diamond — but my father refused. After my father passed away, he asked me for it. He said that he did not want any allowance, instead he requested me to give the diamond. My father warned me about it before he died. So I told him that he could ask for anything else but the diamond, as it would go against my dead father's wish.

He said nothing but I realised that he was very displeased with me. After that I did not meet my uncle.

But I got a letter from him on the day I returned from Calcutta with the diamond after the exhibition. It was a short letter but enough to make me nearly faint with anxiety. Read this letter."

He opened the drawer of the Secretariat Table with his keys and took out a letter. It was written in a beautiful hand.

"Dear Tridib,

Don't be sad. You did not want to give it, so I took it myself. Don't believe in the superstitious story of your family being destroyed if you lose the diamond. It was just a ploy of our ancestors to ensure that it remained with only one branch of the family. God bless you.

Your uncle,
Digindranarayan Roy."

Byomkesh returned the letter silently. Kumar continued, "As soon as I read the letter, I ran to the locker room, opened the vault, took out the box with the diamond and found that it was there. I called the Dewan. He got it checked by an expert, an experienced fellow, who said that it was a mere imitation, but it looked exactly like the original." Kumar opened an almirah and took out a velvet box. The rounded stone reflected the light and sparkled as soon as the lid was opened. Kumar lifted it with two fingers and passed it to Byomkesh, "No one except a jeweler will know the difference. This one costs only about two hundred rupees."

For some time, the two of us looked at the stone, then Byomkesh gave it back to Tridibnarayan and said with a sigh, "So my job is to get back the diamond."

Kumar looked keenly at Byomkesh and said, "Yes. I don't want to know how it was stolen but I want my diamond back at any cost. I am ready to pay any amount for it — don't worry about expenses. But please see that this affair is not leaked to the press."

Byomkesh said casually, "How soon do you want the diamond back?"

Kumar's face shone with happy expectation, "How soon? — that means you are sure to get it back for me?"

Byomkesh smiled, "It is a very simple matter. I expected a much more complicated mystery. Anyhow today is a Saturday, you will get back the diamond by next Saturday," saying this he got up.

After returning to Calcutta we could do nothing on the first day.

We spoke in the evening. "Have you chalked out any plan of campaign?" I asked.

Byomkesh said, "No. Firstly, I will have to see the house and get some information. Only then will I chalk out a plan."

"Is the diamond in the house?"

"Of course. The greed of the diamond made an uncle steal it from his nephew. Is it possible for him to part with it even for a moment? I will only have to find out where he has kept it, I think ...."

"What do you think?"

"No, it is only my guess. I will have to meet old Digindranarayan before I arrive at any conclusion."

I was quiet for some time, then said, "Byomkesh have you considered the moral side of the whole affair?"

"What affair?"

"The way you are going to retrieve the diamond?"

"Yes, I have thought about it. If it was only simple theft — I would be clapped in chains if I am caught. To set a thief to catch a thief is an act of great virtue."

"Maybe, but the laws of the country will not agree to that."

"I am not concerned with that. The lawmakers of the country are free to catch me if they can."

Next afternoon, Byomkesh went out alone and came back late in the evening. Later, I asked him while sipping a cup of tea, "How far have you progressed?"

Distractedly, Byomkesh bit into a *samosa* and said, "Not much. The old man is a hard nut to crack. There is a Nepali *chawkidar* who has an eye like a hawk. Anyhow, the old man wants a secretary — so I gave in two applications."

"Tell me everything."

Sipping his tea, Byomkesh said, "Whatever Kumar Bahadur said was quite true. His uncle is a very shrewd person. The house is like a museum — a collection of beautiful things. He lives alone but there is no dearth of loyal and trusted employees. Firstly, it is difficult to enter the compound — there are four *chawkidars* with guns, at the gate, they ask a thousand questions if you wish to go in. it is impossible to scale the eight feet high surrounding wall which is topped with iron spikes. If you somehow manage to go through the gate by flattering the four watchmen — then you have to face Ujre Singh — the Nepali servant who is sitting at the front door like a ferocious tiger. If you can't give him a convincing excuse to go in — your chances of getting inside are nil. The arrangements at night are even better. The human guards are already there, on top of that are four watchdogs, which are left loose in the compound. So it is impossible to get my work done in the silence of the night."

"Now what?"

"There is a way. The old fellow needs a secretary — he has put in an advertisement — the salary is a thousand rupees and he has to stay in the house. He should be a science graduate and have a knowledge of shorthand and typing and various other good qualities. So I have put in two applications. Tomorrow is the interview."

"Why did you put in two applications?"

"One for you and one for me so that if one of us fails, the other will pass."

Next morning, that is on Monday, we went for an interview at eight in the morning at Sir Digindranarayan's house. His house was in a posh area of south Calcutta. When we pushed our way through the barricade of watchmen, we found that there were quite a few job seekers waiting for their turn. We were made to sit in one room and we looked askance at each other. Byomkesh and I pretended that we did not know each other — that was our plan.

The master of the house was calling each candidate individually from somewhere inside the house. We were worried that someone would be chosen for the job and we would not be called at all. But luckily we found that the disappointed candidates were leaving one after the other, after the interview. The last ones left to be interviewed were Byomkesh and I.

Needless to say we had given false names in our applications. Byomkesh was Nikhilesh and I was Jitendranath. I was mentally reciting my new name in case I should forget it — when a servant came and called both of us together. We were a little surprised. Till now each candidate was being called individually — why were we being called together? Anyway, we followed the servant without a word to the master of the house.

In a huge room, devoid of any furniture except a big secretariat table, Sir Digindranarayan was sitting on a chair behind the table — facing the door. He was a huge man wearing a sleeveless phiran. Can you imagine a bulldog with grizzly beard and moustache? — Well Sir Digindra looked like one. Your first reaction after seeing him would be to turn around and run from the room. His head was like a huge round vessel, there was a bald patch in the center. He had no chin. His huge hairy arms reminded one of a frightening ape, surprisingly his fingers were delicate, slim, long and artistic. His eyes were small and deep-set, aggressively hunting for an adversary to fight. This man who resembled a giant from the Arabian Nights looked as if he had the capacity to do both good and evil. He inspired fear as well as respect.

We humbly paid our obeisance and stood in front of the table. Those small eyes looked from one to the other and fixed on Byomkesh. Then there was a curious smile on the huge face. I don't know if a bulldog smiles — but if it did it would have looked like him. The smile vanished. He ordered in a deep voice, "Ujre, shut the door." The servant did exactly as he was told and went out. The master glanced at our applications on the table and said, "Who is Nikhilesh?"

Byomkesh said, "I am Nikhilesh." The master said, "You are Nikhilesh and you are Jitendranath — you have conspired to apply together?"

Byomkesh said, "Sir, I don't know him."

"Really, you don't know each other? But I came to a different conclusion after reading your applications. Anyway you have passed your M.Sc. exams?"

"Yes, Sir."

"From Calcutta University."

He picked up a thick book the table and said, "Which year?"

Petrified, I realized that the book was the University gazette which had the names of all the successful candidates of the past years. I began perspiring with nervousness — now we will be caught.

But Byomkesh said in a steady voice, "I passed this year, Sir. My results came out about a month back."

I heaved a sigh of relief — the names of this year's candidates were not yet included in the gazette.

The gentleman pushed the book aside and then began cross-questioning Byomkesh. But he could not find any fault or loopholes in his answers. Byomkesh passed the shorthand test easily. The master was pleased and said, "Good, you will serve my purpose. Just sit there."

Byomkesh sat down. Our employer then sat staring at the table with a frown on his forehead. After some time, he suddenly lifted his head, looked at me and said, "Ajitbabu?"

"Yes?"

He burst into laughter like a huge bomb. His body was heaving with uncontrolled laughter. I was puzzled at his sudden burst of amusement and looked at Byomkesh. He was looking at me with an accusing expression. I realised that I had blundered and was full of shame and remorse. I had spoiled everything in a moment with my carelessness.

The gentleman's laughter continued about five minutes, the sound reverberating in the room. He wiped his tears of laughter, and looking at my shame-faced expression, said, "Don't feel so sad — there is no shame in my catching you out. I am surprised and amused that you should even imagine that being so young in maturity and intelligence — you would be able to cheat me."

We were silent. He looked at Byomkesh and said, "I did not expect this stupidity from you — you are young but the shape of your head indicates that you are intelligent." He stared at Byomkesh's head and said, "You have at least fifty five ounces of brain in your skull. But it is not enough just to have brains — everything depends on convolutions. High cheek bones and a prominent jawbone, hooked nose, the shape of the face — all indicate a fast thinker and walker, shrewd and stubborn — a great deal of intuition — well-developed reasoning power but it has not matured yet — yes, more or less intelligent."

I felt that he was doing a post-mortem of a living person. He was dissecting and weighing Byomkesh's brain and I was standing by and observing it.

The gentleman stopped his soliloquy and said, "Do you know how much brain I have? Sixty ounces — five ounces more than you. In other words the difference in the weight of the brain of an ape and a human being — that is the difference between your brain and mine — in fact a bit more."

Byomkesh sat like a statue with a blank expression.

Again Sir Digindra laughed, then suddenly he became serious and said, "I know that my nephew has sent you to steal something from me. Do you think you will succeed?"

Even now Byomkesh did not reply — observing his silence, the gentleman said, "What's wrong Byomkesh, have you forgotten to speak? You have taken up a great task — you tried to disguise yourself to get hold of a great object — so what do you think? Will you succeed?"

Byomkesh said coolly, "I have promised Kumar Bahadur that I will give back his stone to him within seven days."

Digindra's huge face looked frightening — his puckered hairy eyebrows knotted on his forehead.

"Really? You are very bold and cheeky but how will you succeed? I will throw you out of the house right now — then how will you come back?"

Byomkesh smiled and said, "Your words have made something obvious — the diamond is in this house."

His eyes flashing with anger, the master said, "Yes, it is in this house. But will you be able to find it? Do you have that much of intelligence?"

Byomkesh only smiled. This seemed to infuriate the gentleman and he looked as if he was about to burst. The prominent veins on his forehead started throbbing, his eyes gleamed with revenge. If there was any weapon near him — Byomkesh would have been at a great risk of life. Thank God that there was nothing near at hand, so he shook his great head and said, "Look here Byomkeshbabu, you think that you are very intelligent, isn't it? You think that you are the greatest detective this side of the Atlantic? I will not throw you out. You will have complete freedom to come in and to go out of this house. Find out what you have come for. You have given your word that you will find it within seven days. I am giving you seven years — find it if you can and be damned." He stood up, "Ujre Singh!"

Ujre Singh came out at once. The master showed us to him and said, "Look at these two gentlemen — allow them to come into the house even if I am not there. You can move anywhere inside the house — don't stop them."

Ujre Singh looked at us and said, "Yes, Sir." And went out.

Then Sir Digindra roared like a lion, "Finders keepers — have you understood, Byomkesh Chandra."

Byomkesh said, "Sir, only Byomkesh, not Byomkesh Chandra."

"Never mind. You will grow old and die but you will never find the diamond. It is impossible for Byomkesh Bakshi to find what Digin Roy has hidden. If you need the keys to my vaults you just have to ask. I have priceless things in them but I don't distrust you. But I am warning you about one thing — do not destroy my paintings and statues in your eagerness to search for the diamond. If you break or tear or destroy any of my works of art, you will be asked to leave immediately and you will lose your chances of ever getting the diamond."

Pleasing us with such polite and genial conversation — he stomped out of the room. We sat facing each other quietly. Byomkesh was also tired after his tete-e-tete with the old man. His smile was pale when he said, "Let's go back home — nothing can be done today."

It was insulting and demoralising for us to be caught while trying to fool someone — so we went back home unhappy and defeated.

After taking a cup of tea — I recovered a bit and said, "Byomkesh, it is because of my foolishness that you have been insulted like this."

Byomkesh said, "Yes, you were foolish — but that did not alter anything. The old man knew everything right from the beginning. Do you remember that gentleman in the train? The one who said that he would get down at the next stop and got on to the next compartment? He was this gentleman's spy. The old man knows every detail about us."

"He really made a fool of us. This has never happened before."

Byomkesh said after a few minutes of silence, "Thank God that the old man has a terrible weakness, otherwise we would have to give it all up."

I sat up, "How? Do you still have some hope?"

"Of course. Had he thrown us out then it would have been difficult. Anyway, since the old man has shown a weakness — we will have to use it to our advantage to win the day."

"What weakness are you talking about — I saw no chink in his armour — it seemed thick and strong as iron."

"But there is a hole, and a big one at that and through that hole we have managed to enter the house. I don't know why, but these great people are always susceptible to this weakness. The more intelligent they are, the greater is their pride. So sometimes their intelligence goes to waste."

"Why are you talking in riddles — please tell me clearly without insinuations."

"The old man's greatest weakness is his pride in his intelligence. I realised it right at the beginning so I used this to get my work done. Half the battle is won because I have managed to enter the house. Now the only thing left is to find the diamond."

"Are you going there again?"

"Of course, I can't let this chance slip from my hands."

"If you go this time, Ujre Singh will stab you with his dagger. Anyway do whatever you want — I am not in it."

Byomkesh smiled and said, "That's not possible. You have to accompany me — we are in it together."

The next day we went early to Sir Digindra's house. I felt as nervous as a ticketless traveller when we entered the house. But the watchmen said nothing to us. Ujre Singh pretended not to see us. Byomkesh talked to a servant and got to know that the master of the house was in his studio.

Then began our search. Only Byomkesh could dare to look for a small stone in this huge mansion. Anyone else would have been disheartened and would have left the job. It was like looking for a needle in haystack. Firstly, it was useless to search those places like almirahs, cupboards and vaults where precious things are usually kept. The old man was too shrewd to keep the diamond in these obvious places. Then where would it be? I had read a story by Edgar Allan Poe where an important document had been hidden in a very innocuous place.

Byomkesh was not a person to idle away his time. He began a regular search. He tested the walls to see if these were hollow. He took out nearly every book from a huge cupboard. Sir Digindra's house was a virtual art gallery with beautiful paintings and sculptures. Every room had beautiful pictures and statues made of plaster of paris. But the house had very little furniture. It did not take more than two hours to search the whole house. Our search, of course, was fruitless. Lastly we went to the studio where Sir Digindra was working.

We knocked at the door and a deep voice asked us to come in.

The room was large. A table covered one entire side of the room. There were many scientific instruments on the table. As soon as we entered, Sir Digindra roared with laughter, "Hello Byomkeshbabu, did you get your touchstone? You will grow a beard like old Rip Van Winkle by the time you get your stone."

Byomkesh said, "I want to see your steel vault."

Sri Digindra said, "Sure, here take the keys. I would have helped you to look for the diamond. But at present I am busy with this plaster cast. Ajitbabu will help you instead — or maybe Ujre Singh."

Byomkesh stopped his sarcastic comments by asking, "What's that you are doing?"

His smiled slightly and said, "You must have heard about my world famous statues of Nataraj. This is a miniature of the same — there is another one on my table — which you must have seen. Its not bad as a paper weight."

I remember that I had seen an exquisite statue of Nataraj on his table — I realized that, that must be the miniature of his famous Nataraj statue — I said admiringly, "Is that the one you exhibited in Paris?"

He said casually, "Yes the original statue is in stone and at present it is in Louvre."

We came out of the room. This man's versatility impressed me greatly. So when Byomkesh started looking through the vault, I just stood aside. Was it possible to fight a war with this genius?

After his search, Byomkesh sighed and said, "No, nothing here, let's go and sit in the drawing room for sometime."

When we entered the room we found Digindra already there, smoking a cigar proportionate to his size. He looked at Byomkesh and said, "Didn't get it? Never mind, rest a while then begin your search again."

Byomkesh gave back the keys, which Digindra casually put in his pocket and asked me, "Ajitbabu, you are a writer — so you must be appreciating true art and beauty. What do you think of this small statue?" saying this he handed the miniature of Nataraj to me. The statuette was about six inches in height and three inches in circumference. But even within these limits, it was exquisite. Every expression of the Nataraj's dance of destruction was etched on each part of the body of that little statue. I looked at it admiringly and said, "Beautiful, it has no comparison."

Byomkesh asked disinterestedly, "Did you mould it yourself?"

Sir Digindra blew out a mouthful of smoke and said, "Who will do it except me?"

Byomkesh took the statue from me and looked at it, "Is it available in the market?"

Sir Digindra said, "No — why, would you have bought it if it was?"

"Maybe. Why don't you make plaster casts of this statue on a large scale and sell it in the market — I think there is money in such a business."

Annoyed, Digindra said, "If I need money badly, I will take your advice. At present I don't want to cheapen my work of art by selling it in the market."

Byomkesh got up and said, "We will go now and come again in the afternoon." Saying this he kept the statue on the table with a loud thud.

Sir Digindra was at once startled and annoyed, "Are you a fool — you would have broken it just now." Then he looked at Byomkesh like an angry tiger and said, "I have already warned you that if you destroy any of my paintings or statues, you will be thrown out of my house."

Byomkesh looked repentant and said he was sorry for his carelessness. Sir Digindra cooled down, "I can't tolerate negligence of my art pieces. Anyway come in the afternoon — which side of the house will you search this time. If you want to dig up the garden — I will also make arrangements for that. It is good to see you so determined."

We digested his scorn and came out of the house.

Byomkesh said, "Let's go to the National Library."

In the library Byomkesh read the portions on plaster castings, in great detail. I noticed that for some reason he was quite excited. After returning home I asked, "Why are you so curious about plaster casting?"

Byomkesh said, "You know that I am sometimes unnecessarily curious — that is my weakness."

"I know that, but what did you find out?"

"I found out that plaster casting is a very simple thing — anyone can do it. You have to mix some plaster of paris in water and stir it till it becomes thick, then you have to pour it slowly into a mould. Within ten minutes it hardens — and then it is to be taken out from the mould. The only thing which is difficult to make is the mould."

"Why are you so worried about all this."

"No, I am not worried. If a person put in a small rounded stone while pouring the plaster of paris, then it will remain in the statue."

"What do you mean?" Byomkesh looked at me quizzically and said, "Whoever understands will realise."

In the afternoon we again went to Sir Digindra's house. Again we searched the house minutely without any result. Sir Digindra sometimes came to make scornful digs at us. At last, tired, we came to the sitting room and rested a bit. We were served tea and snacks. I was ashamed to take the tea but I found that Byomkesh quite shamelessly consumed everything that was served, while talking to Digindra amiably.

Sir Digindra asked, "For how long are you going to try? Are you not going to give up?"

Byomkesh said, "Today is Wednesday — I have two more days."

Sir Digindra laughed loudly. Byomkesh did not react but picked up the Nataraj statue from the table and said, "When did you make this one?"

Sir Digindra thought for some time and said, "About fifteen or twenty days back — why?"

"No particular reason — we will come tomorrow — goodbye." Byomkesh stood up.

As soon as we returned, Putiram, our servant gave us a letter which he said had been delivered by an uniformed peon. The envelope contained only a visiting card of Kumar

Tridibendra Narayan Roy — on the opposite side was a small note in pencil, "I have arrived just now, putting up at the Grand Hotel, how far have you progressed?"

Byomkesh kept the card aside and sat on the armchair. I realised that he was not happy at the sudden arrival of Kumar Bahadur. When I asked him, he said, "His anxiety may affect the other party. His arrival may make the old man nervous and he may change his plans — then I will have to begin all over again."

Byomkesh relaxed in the armchair the whole evening. We slept in the same room in two separate beds. Usually we chatted for a long time before going off to sleep. But this night, Byomkesh was silent. I spoke in soliloquy for some time and then went off to sleep.

I dreamt that Byomkesh, Sir Digindra and I were playing marbles with diamonds. Byomkesh was winning all the diamonds and Sir Digindra was howling like a little boy. I woke up with a start.

I found Byomkesh sitting by my bed in the dark. When he realised that I was awake he said, "I am sure that the diamond is on the table in the sitting room."

I asked sleepily, "What time of the night is it?"

"2.30 a.m. Did you notice that the old man always glances at the table whenever he enters the room?"

I said, "Maybe, now you close your eyes and go to sleep."

Byomkesh began speaking to himself, "Why does he look at the table? Is it in the drawer? No it is on the table. What are the things there on the table — an ivory inkpot, a small timepiece, a bottle of gum, a few books, blotting pad, a box of cigars, pin cushions, Nataraj ...."

I went off to sleep. Whenever I woke up at night, I found Byomkesh walking up and down the room.

In the morning, Byomkesh wrote a letter to Kumar Tridib and posted it. He was asked not to worry and to wait till Saturday when Byomkesh would meet him.

We went out again. I realised that Byomkesh had come to a conclusion after staying up the whole night.

Sir Digindra was in the sitting room. He welcomed us heartily as soon as he saw us, "Welcome my inseparable friends, you are very early today. Bring tea for the two gentlemen. Byomkesh babu — your face is small and you look tired — could you not sleep due to anxiety?"

Byomkesh picked up the Nataraj from the table and said, "I am in love with this statue — I could not sleep last night because of this."

For a minute, their eyes locked. There seemed to be a silent war between the two. After some time, Sir Digindra laughed and said, "I have understood what you mean, Byomkesh — you can't cheat this old man. You said you couldn't sleep because of this statue — all right, I am presenting it to you."

Byomkesh was truly startled — seeing his expression, the old man said, "Now what? You did not expect this, did you? But don't destroy the statue — it is of great value to me."

Byomkesh recovered in a minute, wrapped the statue in a hanky, put it in his pocket and said, "Thank you."

Then again we continued our fruitless search and returned home. Sitting on the chair, Byomkesh said, "I was wrong."

I said, "What happened? I could understand nothing that passed between the two of you."

Taking out the statue, Byomkesh said, "I was certain after much thought that the diamond was inside this statue. Just think, this was a perfect place to hide the stone. It is in front of everyone's eyes yet no one would suspect anything. Digindranath could easily put the diamond inside while casting it in plaster of paris. Moreover, Digindranath loves the diamond so much that he would always want it near him without raising anyone's suspicion. So I was positive that the diamond was in the statue and I was going to challenge the old man into admitting it. But I was wrong. Not only did the old man realise what I was thinking of — but my whole theory has gone for a toss. To pile insult to injury, the old fellow gave me the statue as a present! Now I will have to begin my investigation all over again."

I said, "There is no time now — there is only one day left."

Byomkesh turned the statue and wrote his initials below it in pencil and said, "Yes, only one day left. I don't think I will be able to keep my promise. Kumar is already in Calcutta. This old man is really making me a laughing stock." Saying this Byomkesh kept the statue on the table and sat with his head bent.

In the afternoon, as usual, Byomkesh and I went to the house of Sir Digindra. We learnt that the master had gone out. Byomkesh tried a new device — he asked me to go away so that he could have a friendly chat with Ujre Singh. I wandered around the garden and noticed Ujre Singh and Byomkesh talking. It was true that Byomkesh could easily gain the confidence of people. But I doubted if he would be able to thaw the Himalayan ice of the Nepali Ujre Singh. After two hours when the two of us came out of that house, Byomkesh said, "My efforts were useless, either Ujre Singh is very stupid or much more intelligent than I am."

After returning home, we were informed by our servant that someone had waited for us for half an hour and then left saying that he would come back. Byomkesh said tiredly, "That must have been Kumar's man."

I was tired of the whole business and told Byomkesh, "Leave this case — this time you will have to admit defeat. Tell Kumar Saheb that you are sorry, why keep him hoping?"

Sitting at the table, Byomkesh was playing with the Nataraj and said, "Let's see — we still have tomorrow." Before he could complete his sentence, I found that the expression on his face had changed to one of intense excitement. He was staring at the Nataraj.

"What happened?" I asked.

With trembling hands, Byomkesh passed the statue to me and said, "Look, you must remember that I had written my initials at the bottom — this statue does not have it."

I saw that it was not there but what was there to get so excited about? The initials were written in pencil — it could have been rubbed off.

Byomkesh said, "Can't you understand?" he laughed loudly, "What a fool the old man has made of us! But a giant has a giant killer too. Putiram!" he called.

When our servant, Putiram came, Byomkesh asked, "Where did the gentleman, who waited for us, sit?"

"In this room, sir."

"Were you here with him all the time?"

"Yes, but in between he asked for a glass of water so ...."

"O.K. you may go."

Byomkesh smiled quietly to himself, "You will be surprised to know that the diamond was here on my table from morning till this evening."

I was surprised — has Byomkesh gone out of his mind?

I heard him talking to Tridibendra Narayan over the phone, "You will get your diamond by 10 o'clock tomorrow morning. Your special train should be ready. As soon as you get the thing, you should start — it is not safe for you to stay here with the thing. Please see that you leave Calcutta by 10. All right, I will arrange for the special train. Don't say anything to anyone — not even to your secretary."

Then he went out, probably to arrange for a special train — he told me to take my dinner and go to bed because he would be late. I don't know when Byomkesh returned. Next morning, at eight thirty, we went out as usual. I noticed that the Nataraj statue was not in its place on our table — when I asked Byomkesh, he only said, "I have kept it."

Sir Digindra was in his sitting room. He saw us and said, "You have become a habit with me — I have learnt to wait for you to come."

Byomkesh said apologetically, "We have given you a lot of trouble — we won't anymore — that is what we have come to tell you. In a game like this one has to lose and the other will win — it is no use feeling sorry for it, it is better to accept it. You won't see us from tomorrow. You already know that your nephew is here. Yesterday I told him to leave Calcutta — I will give him my final answer today."

Sir Digindra stared at Byomkesh, then he smiled again like a bulldog and said, "I am glad that you have come to your senses. Tell my nephew not to waste his time."

"All right," Byomkesh picked up another Nataraj statue from the table and said, "You have made a new one. I have kept your gift with great care. Not only because it is beautiful but because it will be a souvenir of your memory. If it breaks — will I get another one?"

Sir Digindra was pleased, "Yes, you will get another one. You have learnt to appreciate art in my house — that is a great thing.

With great humility, Byomkesh said, "Really, all these past years, that area of my mind had been covered with a dark curtain. It was in your presence that I began to appreciate art, I have realised what invaluable, priceless matter is hidden in art. I like that painting behind you — have you done that too?" It was a beautiful painting — Sir Digindra turned his head to look at it. In a second Byomkesh showed tremendous sleight of hand by exchanging the Nataraj on the table with the one in his pocket. When Sir Digindra turned his face — Byomkesh was looking admiringly at the painting. Sir Digindra said, "Yes, I have done it." My heart began thumping with excitement — I heard his voice from a distance — I was lucky that he did not look at my expression — he would surely have caught us out then.

Byomkesh got up slowly and said, "We will leave now. I have benefitted after coming in contact with you — I will never forget that. I hope you too won't forget me. I am a truth seeker — my hobby and my passion is to find out the truth. If you ever need me, I will be only too eager to help you. Come Ajit. Goodbye, Sir."

I turned around to see that Sir Digindra was looking at Byomkesh quizzically — half-aware of Byomkesh's innuendoes.

We caught a taxi and began driving to Grand Hotel.

I caught Byomkesh by the hand and said, "What is happening?"

Byomkesh smiled, "Didn't you understand? My assumption that the diamond was in the Nataraj was correct. The old man understood and to puzzle me, presented me with that very statue. Then he made another one exactly like the first and exchanged it with the one he had given me in my own house. I would not have understood anything if I had not scribbled my initials at the bottom of the statue." He turned the statue and showed me the faded initials. "When I found that my initials were not there under the statue, last evening, I realised that it has been exchanged. Everything became clear. Later you saw the trick I played to exchange the statue in the presence of Sir Digindra."

"Are you sure that the diamond is in this statue? What if it isn't?"

"If it isn't, then I will think that there is nothing called logic or conjecture or truth in this world."

In the hotel, Kumar Bahadur said, "This is Uncle's Nataraj — where's my diamond?"

"It is inside the statue."

"I can't understand anything — are you sure?" said a visibly impatient Kumar.

Byomkesh struck the statue with a paperweight — it broke into pieces. Byomkesh picked up the diamond from the crumbled pieces of plaster of paris and handed it to the gentleman — "Take your diamond."

Although some broken pieces of plaster were still sticking to it — it could easily be recognised as a priceless object, even by amateurs.

Kumar Bahadur virtually snatched the diamond from Byomkesh's hand — stared at it and said delightedly, "Yes, this is my diamond — I don't know how to thank you. Look at it — it is giving off a light blue ray."

Byomkesh said, "Now you leave Calcutta as fast as you can. If your uncle discovers that the diamond is with you — he will make another plan."

"No, no, I will leave just now — but your fees?"

"Pay me later — first you must reach home safely."

We took Kumar to the station, came back home and relaxed in our room. Byomkesh said smilingly, "I just want to know what the old man will do when he discovers the loss."

After a few days, we received a registered envelope from Kumar Bahadur. A cheque was attached to a letter from him.

"Dear Byomkeshbabu,

I am sending you this small sum as a token of my eternal gratitude — please accept it although I know that it is a pittance in comparison to your talent. I am looking forward to meeting you in the near future. The next time I go to Calcutta, I will get to know from you all that had happened. Please thank Ajitbabu for me — he is a writer. I don't want to insult his art by offering him money. (Oh! Hapless writer!). If he wishes to write the story of this diamond by changing names and places, then I will not object.

My respects
Yours admiringly,
Sir Tridibendra Narayan Roy.

The Avenger
(Achin Pakhi)

Byomkesh and I went to Birenbabu's daughter's wedding last February. The town was some distance away from Calcutta. It was ancient and dirty. From Calcutta It took us about three hours by train.

We knew Birenbabu intimately for a long time. He was a police officer in Calcutta. An amiable and helpful man, he had retired two years back and had settled here in his ancestral home. He had begged us to attend his daughter's wedding. Byomkesh was free, so we decided to accept the invitation.

As we reached the house, we heard the sound of "shehnai" and saw people busily running here and there. Birenbabu welcomed us warmly and took us to a decorated room, which the bridegroom with his entourage would occupy in the evening. At present it was empty. We made ourselves comfortably there and were served tea and snacks. Byomkesh told Birenbabu, "You must be very busy, feel free to go and attend to your duties. We are very comfortable."

Birenbabu looked relieved. Suddenly we heard a deep voice outside, "Biren, I have come to see what arrangements you have made for your daughter's wedding."

Birenbabu quickly went out and ushered an elderly man into the room, "It is good, Sir, that you have come. These are my two friends from Calcutta. He is the well-known Byomkesh Bakshi, the Truth Seeker and this is his famous writer-friend — Ajit Banerjee."

"Yes, indeed, I have heard of them." The old gentleman gave us a sharp glance.

Birenbabu said, "He is Neelmani Majumdar. Also a well-known police officer. He has settled here after retirement."

He was a tall and fair man, well above sixty but erect as a ramrod. Although he had a walking stick in his hand — he did not seem to need it. His voice was heavy and his appearance commanded respect.

Byomkesh asked him to sit down. Birenbabu sought our permission to leave. Byomkesh asked, "Is your ancestral home here, too?"

Neelmanibabu said, "No, my home was in East Bengal — but everything was lost during Partition. After retirement I have settled here."

Byomkesh asked, "Do you have relatives here?"

Neelmanibabu said, "I have no relatives. I am a bachelor. I was so involved with the police job that I did not think of anything else. Then when I retired, I remained here. I have an affection for this town. When I started my career as a sub-inspector, I was posted here. Before I retired, I was posted here, too."

Byomkesh smiled, "You love this town. How long have you been retired?"

"Seven years."

As in most cases, Byomkesh was the subject of Neelmanibabu's curiosity. But his glance was different from the admiring glances of other people. He seemed to be weighing and gauging Byomkesh and his intelligence.

When he spoke, he sounded skeptical and at the same time curious, "Byomkeshbabu, I have read about you and your work. I have noticed that you have solved all the cases which have come to you. So I am curious to know, have you never been unsuccessful? Have you never made a mistake?"

Byomkesh smiled humbly, "I can't say I have never made mistakes or I have never failed. In fact I have even failed to catch criminals in a few cases. But I have always got to the bottom of the mystery and found out the truth. Sir, remember that I am a truth seeker. But, of course, you must have had many more cases than I have ever had."

Neelmanibabu seemed quite satisfied with Byomkesh's answer. He now sounded a bit more friendly. "Look there are a lot of problems in our job. Most of the cases are small ones dealing with petty criminals. It is rarely that we get cases involving big criminals. Again, my experience says that it is easier to catch the bigger offenders than the small ones."

Byomkesh said, "Even the doctors say that it is easier to cure serious diseases rather than common cold. So, have you been successful in catching all your important offenders?"

Neelmanibabu was quiet for some time. Then he looked at Byomkesh sharply.

"I have been successful in most cases, except the last case of my life. It happened in this town itself. But I could not solve it."

Byomkesh said, "You know who the culprit was but could not prove it — is that so?"

Neelmanibabu said hesitantly, "I was sure that one particular person was involved but I could not break his alibi. Then another incident occurred which turned all my investigations topsy turvy. I never could find out who the real culprit was."

Byomkesh was quiet. Neelmani Majumdar looked at Byomkesh sharply and said, "Do you want to hear the story?"

Byomkesh said eagerly, "Of course, it seems a very interesting one."

"You will judge whether it was interesting. I will tell you all I know about the case. Maybe you will succeed where I had failed!"

There was a note of challenge in his voice. Byomkesh smiled and said, "I don't think it is possible for me to solve something which an experienced person like you could not. I am only interested in hearing the story."

Neelmani Majumdar began his story in his deep resonant voice: —

Just before retirement, Neelmanibabu was posted in this town as the head of the police station here. He had three good qualities, intelligence, diligence and honesty — he never took bribes. This town, though small, was known for its criminal activities. Neelmani knew this town well, so after being transferred here, he took up the reins of police administration with iron hands.

A year and a half passed. There was some peace in this town, thanks to Neelmani. He had a habit of going on rounds twice a week at midnight on his cycle. No one knew when he would go on these rounds. One part of the town was especially prone to crimes. This part was a special favourite with Neelmani. He used to move around the small lanes and by-lanes and kept a watch on whether the policemen on duty were alert. There were no lights in his cycle but he always had his revolver and a torch with him.

On this particular night, he was on his usual rounds. It was a dark night and no one was around. There was an area in-between the place which housed well-to-do, decent society and the dark lanes of the criminal world. This area was a twilight area, surrounded by mango groves. It consisted of a few dilapidated houses. The people of this area too belonged neither here nor there.

While moving in this area, Neelmani noticed that about fifty yards away a few men were carrying something like a bamboo cot on their shoulders. Their behaviour was suspicious.

He quickly rode up to them and accosted them by flashing his torch on their faces, "Stop!"

There were four people, they dropped the cot and vanished in the dark. But Neelmani clearly saw the face of one of them. He was the owner of one of those houses — Sureshwar Ghose.

The men had vanished in all directions — it was useless following them. Neelmani went up to the cot and found that on it was the body of a young, healthy woman — there was no sign of wounds but she was dead.

Neelmani blew his whistle. Slowly policemen and people began collecting there. The neighbours identified the body immediately — it was Hashi — the wife of Sureshwar. No one else lived in the house besides Sureshwar and his wife.

Neelmani took a few neighbours with him and entered the house. It was quite a large house with about six rooms. But most of the rooms were not used. Only two rooms were used — one was the bedroom. It was a large room with two beds. One looked slept in — the other was not. But there was no one in the house. There was no one in the garden either. There were mango and jackfruit trees in the garden. Neelmanibabu asked the neighbours, "Was the girl ill?"

One of them said, "No, this afternoon I saw her talking to Binodbabu, near the gate."

"Who is Binodbabu?"

"Binod Sarkar — he is a jeweller and has a shop in the market."

Some more constables had arrived with the sub-inspector — he sent the body with them for post-mortem.

The neighbours were still standing around, gossiping and whispering to each other. Neelmani asked them, "What is the name of the girl's husband?"

"Sureshwar Ghose."

"Where is he?"

No one opened his mouth. Then one person said unwillingly, "Sureshwar goes out of the house after dinner and does not come back till one thirty or two in the night."

"Where does he go?"

"We've heard that he goes to Kalikinkar Das's shop to gamble."

"Where is Kalikinkar Das's shop?"

The neighbours gave him the address. Neelmani left a constable waiting in the house and took the sub-inspector with him to look for the shop. He told the neighbours, "I will come and take your testimony tomorrow morning."

Kalikinkar's shop was half a mile from Sureshwar's house — just near the edge of the market place. It was an iron and steel shop. This area of the market was known as 'Lohapatty'.

Neelmani reached his shop, walking through the deserted market place. Iron rods were heaped in front of the shop. But the door of the shop was closed. Neelmanibabu looked around and then peeped through a hole in the window.

On a carpet on the floor sat four men, playing cards with great concentration. In the middle, was some money. They were obviously gambling for a stake. They were playing flush.

Neelmani beckoned the sub-inspector. The latter stood at the door, while Neelmani knocked at the window. All four turned anxious eyes on the window. One of them grabbed all the money in the center and put it into his pocket.

Neelmani called out in a stern voice, "Open the door."

The four looked at each other and one of them raised his voice and asked, "Who is it?"

Neelmani said, "Police, open the door."

Again they looked at each other, then probably Kalikinkar Das got up. Now Neelmani moved away from the window and stood in front of the door. The door opened. The thin, skeletal man looked at the two police officials and took a step backward, "What? What do you want?"

Neelmani said, "Are you Kalikinkar Das?"

"Yes, what do you want?"

"Who else are there with you?"

Kalikinkar gulped and said, "Three of my friends."

Neelmani entered the shop with the sub-inspector. Next to this room was the door to the office of the shop. When he entered the office, Neelmani found that the three men were still playing cards. He watched each of them. Their ages ranged from thirty-five to forty. Their appearances were undistinguished. Only the one who was serving the cards looked quite muscular. He looked like their leader.

Neelmanibabu asked, "Who is Sureshwar Ghose?"

The stout man looked up, put away the pack of cards and stood up. "I am Sureshwar Ghose, what do you want?" His voice was calm and he was totally composed.

Neelmani looked from one to the other. "You thought that you would take the dead body quietly in the dead of the night and burn it in the ghat? Once it was burnt, there would be no proof of the crime?"

All four looked genuinely surprised. Sureshwar said, "Dead body, whose dead body?"

Neelmanibabu said, "Don't pretend. I saw you in the light of the torch. You are one of the four, who was carrying the dead body."

Sureshwar said, "Which day are you talking about?"

"I am talking about today — tonight at twelve."

"You are talking rubbish. We started playing cards at 8.30 pm. in the evening and none of us went out even for a minute."

"So, you were playing cards — gambling?"

The three looked down guiltily. Sureshwar was bold, "Yes we were gambling. The four of us sometimes play together."

Neelmani found that it was impossible to get anything out of them here; they had to be taken to the police station. He said, "Right now I am arresting you on charges of gambling. Come with us to the police station."

There was an argument but at last all four agreed to go to the police station. Neelmanibabu said, "If you can get a bail, I will let you go tonight."

On the way to the police station, Sureshwar asked, "What were you saying about a dead body? Whose dead body?"

Neelmani said, "Your wife's."

Sureshwar stood stock still on the road, "My wife's? What are you saying?"

"I am saying that your wife has been murdered."

"No, no, I don't believe all this — Hashi — no, I am going home."

"It's no use going home, the dead body has been sent for post-mortem."

In the police station, Neelmanibabu began questioning the four separately. First he called Sureshwar. When he sat down, Neelmani asked, "What work do you do?"

Sureshwar said, "I look after different kinds of business. I am a moneyed man not a petty businessman."

"Is the house yours?"

"Yes."

"When did you buy it?"

"About five or six years back."

"When did you get married?"

"Seven years back."

"Where is your in-laws' house?"

"In this town."

"What is the name of your father-in-law?"

"Dinamani Haldar."

"Where is he now?"

"I am not sure — probably in jail."

"Jail?"

"Yes — jail is where he spends most of his time."

"Do you have a good relationship with your father-in-law?"

"I can't stand him."

Neelmanibabu thought for some time and asked, "Did you have a good relationship with your wife?"

Sureshwar hesitated for a while and said, "As good a relationship as is possible after seven years of marriage."

"Do you have no children?"

"No, my wife was infertile."

Neelmanibabu lifted his finger at him and said, "At twelve tonight I saw you and your three friends carrying the dead body of your wife. I flashed my torch on your face."

Sureshwar said in an unperturbed voice, "You are wrong. I was playing cards in Kalikinkar's shop with three of my friends at twelve."

"What was the character of your wife like?"

"Who can say about the characters of women — but the neighbours spoke ill of her."

"What did they say?'

"I return late at night. It seems a person used to come and meet Hashi for the last few months."

"Did you ask your wife about this?"

"Yes. She said that it was all lies."

"Anything else?"

"What else? Once I opened her cupboard and found a few pieces of jewellery which I had not given her."

"Did you ask where those pieces came from?"

"What's the use? If a woman wants to go astray, no one can save her."

"But one can murder her."

"I have not killed Hashi."

Neelmani tried hard but could not make Sureshwar confess anything. In fact it seemed that he was outspoken and truthful.

Next he called Kalikinkar. The latter had a hard, strong heart in a thin, infirm body. Neelmani could not make him confess either. According to him the four friends had started playing cards at eight thirty in the evening and were there till the police entered the shop. But he was also quite frank. Sureshwar was his childhood friend. Sureshwar was not very rich earlier but had made money through contracts during the war. He had married Hashi when he was poor. Hashi's father was a thief and a fool. He always got caught when stealing and spent a lot of his time in the prison. Hashi's mother had a bad name — living in the slum had corrupted her character. When Hashi's father was in the jail — her mother entertained customers. So when Sureshwar wanted to marry Hashi — all his friends had advised him against it. But he did not listen to anyone. Then Sureshwar became quite rich, bought a house but by that time the relationship between him and his wife had soured. He never stayed home for long but spent most of his time outside. But it is not true that he had murdered his wife. He was not that kind of a person. He came from a good family and had struggled a lot in his early life. But he had a heart of gold. Neelmani asked at this point, "Where is Sureshwar's father-in-law, Dinamani Haldar now?"

Kalikinkar said, "About two years back, Dinamani Haldar came in search of his daughter — his wife was dead. He lived with his daughter and son-in-law for two or three days. One day he had a quarrel with Sureshwar — then Dinamani left. I haven't seen him again. He was old, besides jail life had weakened him — he must be dead."

Next was Debu Mondol's turn. Debu did business in coal and firewood. He was a wealthy man. Sureshwar was a very good childhood friend. It was a total lie that Sureshwar had murdered his wife and was taking her body away to be burnt. They were playing cards. He refused to comment on the character of Hashi — but the girl did not come from a good family.

Neelmani said, "Do you have a shop of firewood in the burning ghat?"

Debu was a little shaken, "Yes, I have two godowns in the town and one in the burning ghat."

Neelmanibabu looked at him with a frown and said, "Will you tell me the truth now?"

"I am telling the truth."

The fourth person was Bilash Dutta — a building contractor — very sweet-tongued, polite and witty. But he, too, had no doubt that the four of them were playing cards from eight thirty in the evening till the police came in. Neelmani found out that Bilash Dutta belonged to that category of human beings who talked a lot of rubbish but never the truth.

Disappointed, he asked, "You are a contractor, you must be having a lot of bamboos."

Bilash said, "Bamboos, yes — lots of bamboos. I need them for scaffoldings for buildings."

"You need them also to make cots for the dead."

It was early morning by the time Neelmanibabu finished questioning the four. But he could not keep them in custody because their lawyer bailed them out the very next day.

Neelmani was sure that Sureshwar had killed his wife but was unable to prove it. He was also sure that the other three were involved. But there was no proof. There was no witness to what he had seen. Their lawyer would prove him wrong in the court. So he could not bring the charge of murder — although he did bring the charge of gambling against them.

But he continued investigating the case. He questioned Sureshwar's neighbours, two of his assistants. Then he went to his house at about one in the afternoon. There was a constable at the gate who said that Sureshwar had come back at eleven and was in the house.

Neelmanibabu entered the house and found him sleeping in one bed. He opened bloodshot eyes at the sound of footsteps and mumbled sleepily, "Now what do you want?"

Neelmanibabu said, "We want to search the house."

"Do whatever you want — let me sleep." He was probably making up for a sleepless night. But did he not feel anything for his wife? Even if he did not murder her — this seemed a strange reaction to Neelmanibabu who was angry at his callous behaviour.

He did not allow Sureshwar to sleep. "I want to see your wife's ornaments."

Sureshwar got up irritatedly, opened the cupboard and took out a box of ornaments. Neelmani said, "Which ones out of there did you not give her?"

Sureshwar picked up a ring, a pair of earrings and a hairclip from the box. Neelmani took them and put them in his pocket, "I am taking these. I will return them later."

Then the police party searched the whole house and garden. But they found nothing incriminating.

At about three in the afternoon, Neelmanibabu went from Sureshwar's house to the shop of Binod Sarkar — the jeweller.

It was a large shop. On one side the workers sat making ornaments. Binod was sitting in a well-decorated room. He was about fifty but had fancy tastes. He wore a silk kurta, a fine quality dhoti, and had a well-trimmed moustache. He tried to hide his bald pate by covering it with hair from all the sides. He was short and a bit plump. When he saw policemen at his doorstep he was slightly nervous. "Has anything happened in my shop? What has happened?"

Neelmani sat on a chair opposite him and said, "No, I have come to get some information from you." "Yes?"

"Sureshwar's wife is dead. Do you know anything about it?"

Binodbabu jumped up from his chair, "Hashi is dead? But I saw her last evening."

"She died last night."

"But she was all right in the evening. How did she die?"

"I think she was murdered."

"Murdered!" Binodbabu sat on his chair and stared vacantly. Then he slapped the table and said, "Sureshwar has killed her, I am sure."

"But Sureshwar has a perfect alibi."

"I don't care about alibi. He and his three friends killed the girl. They are all wicked. They can do anything."

Neelmanibabu said, "Did you know Hashi for a long time?"

"I knew her from when she was three or four years old." Then he gave Neelmani a furtive, shy look and said in a low voice, "You are a policeman, I will not conceal anything from you. When I was young, I had a relationship with Hashi's mother. That was about twenty years ago. Hashi's father was a scoundrel, thief, smuggler, drunkard. He could not feed his wife and daughter. So because of poverty she had to... let that be. A few years ago, Hashi's mother died. Before her death she told me to look after her daughter, as Sureshwar was a wicked person. I could not avoid her last request. So I used to go to the house to meet Hashi. Hashi's mother was not the model of fidelity — that's true — but she was a good human being. She had a very sweet nature."

No one spoke for some time. Then Neelmanibabu said, "Then you suspect that Sureshwar has murdered Hashi?"

Binodbabu surfaced from a sea of memories and said absent mindedly, "What? Yes, I think so."

"But what was his motive?"

"Look, when Sureshwar married Hashi he was a poor man. Then during the war he became very rich. Now he wanted to be associated with respectable people. But if Hashi was alive, it was impossible. Everyone knew what kind of a family Hashi came from. So he killed her. He will marry again and become a gentleman."

"What was Hashi's character and conduct like?"

"She was a simple girl without any hypocrisy or cunning. She may have been a little fond of male company; she would stand at the gate in the evenings and call people and talk to them. One can't blame her — the women in the neighbourhood avoided her for her antecedents — so she too needed company. I can say with conviction that she had no other serious fault of character."

Neelmanibabu then took out Hashi's ornaments from his pocket, "Can you recognise these?"

"Are these Hashi's ornaments? But I have never seen her wearing them."

"You never presented her with ornaments?"

"No, I gave her sarees during the *Pujas* and *Holi*. I never gave her any ornaments."

Neelamnibabu said, "Have these been made in your shop?"

Binodbabu examined them, "No, these have not been made in my shop. Just a minute —," he called a worker, "Please send Ramdayal to me."

An old man came to him; Binodbabu showed him the ornaments. "Did we make these, Ramdayal?"

He looked at them carefully and said, "No, Sir, these have been made in Calcutta."

"Alright, you can go."

Neelmani got up to leave. "I will come again if I need you."

"Most certainly."

That evening Neelmanibabu met the civil surgeon in his bungalow. His office was on one side of the house. Major Burman was winding up his work when Neelmani arrived, "I came to find out about the report."

Major Burman said, "Sit down, I have done the post-mortem. You will get the report tomorrow."

"What did you find out? When did she die?"

"She died at about ten at night."

"How did she die?"

"There was no sign of any assault on her body."

"Was it poison then?"

Major Burman said slowly, "No, not even poison. She was killed in a novel way. Is there any military man among your suspects?"

Neelmani said, "No, but the girl's husband was a military contractor during the war and had worked closely with the American soldiers posted here. Why, what's the matter?"

Major Burman said, "One can't see any sign of a blow anywhere in the body but the thyroid cartilage in her throat was completely broken."

Neelmani said, "That means she was throttled to death."

"No, if she was throttled, there would have been marks of fingers on her throat."

"Then?"

Major Burman said, "In the last war the soldiers were taught to fight without arms."

"How's that?"

"Suppose that a battle was going on in the jungle. You are unarmed and cannot defend yourself and you have been captured by an armed enemy soldier. You are unable to escape — if you try, he will shoot you. So what do you do? Cunningly, you move to the right of your enemy and suddenly you turn round and hit him hard on the throat with the side of your right palm. The thyroid cartilage breaks and the person dies at once — something like your modern karate chop."

"Instant death?"

"Yes."

Neelmanibabu said, "You are sure that the girl was killed like that?"

"I am certain."

"Alright, tomorrow I will send a person for the report."

Neelmani came back to the police station without a doubt in his mind that Sureshwar had killed Hashi. There was only one mystery. Who used to come and meet Hashi at night? Did he give the ornaments? What relation did Hashi have with this man? But if he was Hashi's friend — why should he kill Hashi?

The next day, Neelmanibabu went with a sub-inspector and a constable to Sureshwar's house. He was determined to get a confession out of him.

Sureshwar's house was wide open and there was no one in the house. He called out a few times and went in.

He stopped short when he reached the bedroom. Sureshwar was lying dead on the floor.

The evening before too, Sureshwar had gone to his friend's house to play cards and had come back at about midnight. Then no one knows what had happened.

Major Burman gave the post-mortem report of Sureshwar's body. He too had died because his thyroid cartilage had been broken with a blow. Hashi and Sureshwar were killed in the same way.

After finishing the story, Neelmanibabu stopped for some time — waiting for Byomkesh to ask some questions.

"I have told you everything I know. At first I thought that Sureshwar had killed Hashi. But later, Sureshwar was killed in the same way. So the man who murdered Hashi must have killed Sureshwar also. Can you guess anything?"

Byomkesh was listening attentively, "I want to ask a few more questions."

"I will give you answers if I know the answers myself."

Byomkesh said, "Who is Sureshwar's heir?"

"A cousin of Sureshwar — he had not made a will. She is a widow and penniless. She has got all his property."

"Where were his three friends on the night of his death?"

"After Sureshwar left for home, they played cards nearly for the whole night in Kalikinkar's shop. I had employed informers to bring me all the news. They did not kill Sureshwar."

"What about Binod Sarkar?"

"No, I did not suspect him — what was his motive? He was genuinely fond of Hashi."

"Where was Dinamani Haldar at that time?"

"He was suffering from a terrible attack of dysentery in a village fifty miles away. He could not move. Besides how would he know the trick of killing in that special way?"

"Alright. Do you think that Hashi had a loose character?"

"No, I think she was a good girl."

Byomkesh thought for some time, "But she was born of another with a loose character — what did you say her name was?"

"Amala."

Byomkesh looked up and stared at Neelmanibabu. He too, looked at Byomkesh and his body stiffened. Then Byomkesh relaxed in his chair.

Neelmani said, "Do you want to know anything else?"

Byomkesh said disinterestedly, "There is nothing else to know."

Neelmani said sarcastically, "Have you understood anything?"

Byomkesh said gravely, "Neelmanibabu, I have understood everything."

Neelmani was still for sometime. "You have understood who killed Hashi?"

"Yes, of course. Hashi was murdered by Sureshwar."

"Really? Then who killed Sureshwar?"

"Sureshwar was killed by Hashi's father."

"Hashi's father? But I told you just now that Dinamani Haldar was ill, fifty miles away."

"I am not talking about Dinamani Haldar. I am talking about Hashi's real father, her natural father."

Neelmani was very quiet. I found that he had become very pale. When he spoke again, his voice was a mere whisper, "Natural father? Who do you mean?"

Byomkesh shook his head sadly, "You know who I am talking about, Neelmanibabu. You should not have told me this story."

I don't know how Neelmanibabu would have reacted to this, but at that moment Birenbabu came into the room.

"Byomkeshbabu, lunch is ready. Please have your bath. Neelmanida, why don't you stay back for lunch, too?"

Neelmanibabu stood up hastily, "No, no, I am going. I am already late."

He went out of the room quickly, without once looking back at us.

After lunch, we were relaxing again in the same room.

I asked, "How did you guess about Neelmanibabu?"

Byomkesh said, "While listening to his story I felt that he was favourably inclined towards Hashi, although there was no reason to be so. According to him he did not know Hashi when she was alive. Whatever we got to know about Hashi from his story showed her to be a flirt, her husband was suspicious about her, an unknown man used to visit her at night. Then why should Neelmanibabu be well-disposed towards her?

Hashi's mother was not an example of true fidelity either! Amala's husband Dinamani Haldar was more often inside the prison than not. So Hashi's father may not have been Dinamani.

Binod Sarkar was also not Hashi's father, because he met her mother, Amala, when Hashi was about three or four years old. Then who was the unknown man?

"Neelmani told us even before he began his story that his first posting was in this town. Dinamani was a professional thief. Neelmanibabu may have gone to Amala and Dinamani's house either to search it or to arrest him. It was then that the young policeman had a relationship with the attractive wife of the thief.

"After a year or two, Neelmani was transferred from this place. By this time he had got to know that he had a daughter from Amala and she was called Hashi. He used to keep in touch with Hashi and her mother even when he was posted to other places. He had not married — so the only blood relation he had was Hashi. Towards the end of his career he was again posted in this town. Hashi's mother was dead by that time and she was married. Neelmanibabu had a habit of moving around at night on his cycle to keep vigil. It was during these times that he met Hashi and even presented her with a few pieces of jewellery. She may or may not have known about her relationship with him. But she may have guessed. But her neighbours jumped to the wrong conclusions and thought that she used to meet her paramour at night, in the absence of her husband.

"On the day that Hashi was murdered, Neelmani was probably going to meet her. Then we know what happened from the story he related to us. I think Sureshwar killed his wife and asked his friends to help him that night to burn the body. The friends decided that they would leave no trace of the body and the next day they would tell everyone that Hashi had eloped. They were indeed fast friends!

"Neelmani brought all the four to the police station but failed to find a chink in their alibi. When he found that he was unable to hang the murderer of his daughter, he decided to kill Sureshwar himself to avenge the death of Hashi. He did not wait, within twenty four hours of Hashi's death he killed Sureshwar in the same way as Sureshwar had killed Hashi. He had learnt the art of killing without arms, from what he had heard from the doctor.

"But just think, Ajit, whatever I have told you is based entirely on supposition! I could only be sure if I had any way of proving that Neelmani was Hashi's father. So I set a trap for him. Suddenly I asked, 'What was the name of Hashi's mother?'

"He answered without thinking, 'Amala.' How did he know her name? No one had mentioned her name even once in connection with this case. She had died ten years ago. I had no doubts left now. As soon as he mentioned Amala's name to me, he realised that he had walked into my trap. I, too, realised from the expression on his face that my suspicion was correct. Neelmanibabu's unknown culprit was Neelmanibabu himself."

The Man in a Red Coat
(Chhalanar Chanda)

❧❀❧

Byomkesh spoke into the phone, "Hello?"

The police inspector Rakhalbabu's voice was heard at the other end, "Byomkeshbabu, I am Rakhal. I am calling you up from Netaji Hospital. Could you please come here for a while?"

"What's wrong?"

"Attempt to murder — someone had tried to shoot a man dead — but did not succeed. Now that injured man has been brought to the hospital. He is relating a strange story."

"Really? I am coming."

Byomkesh had moved to his new house in Keyatala — Netaji hospital was not very far from his house. About half an hour later, at about five in the evening, Byomkesh reached the place and found Rakhal standing near the Emergency Ward.

He revealed many details about the case while standing there. The name of the injured person was Gangapada Choudhury. A good man. He was found unconscious on the first floor of a house in a lane off Fraser Road. The part time servant had come in at three in the afternoon and discovered him. It was this servant who had informed the police and the hospital. Gangapada had regained his consciousness but he was weak because he had lost a lot of blood.

Gangapada was looking out of his first floor window, which overlooked a lane, when a bullet grazed his skull and slipped over the skull-bone instead of piercing it.

The bullet was found inside the room. Shot from a revolver it had now been sent for examination. Rakhal took Byomkesh to the man. He had received a blood transfusion and was feeling much better.

Gangapada Choudhury was lying in a small narrow room, on an iron bed. A big bandage covered his head like a turban. His face was thin and longish. He looked pale probably due to the loss of blood. He was about thirty-five. He looked a good and simple person.

Byomkesh and Rakhalbabu pulled up two chairs on either side of his bed and sat down. Gangapada looked once at Byomkesh and then at Rakhalbabu. There was a faint smile on his pale lips. The man had fortunately returned from death's door, but there was no sign of fear in his expression.

Rakhalbabu said, "This is Byomkesh Bakshi. He has come to hear your story."

Gangapada's face lit up, he tried to sit up on his bed quickly. Byomkesh gently pushed him down on his pillows, "Don't get up, lie down."

Gangapada folded his hands in greeting and said in an awestruck voice, "You are the Truth Seeker — Byomkesh Bakshi. My visit to Calcutta has been worthwhile."

Rakhalbabu said, "If you are feeling stronger please relate your story to Byomkeshbabu. But if you are still feeling weak — we will come later."

Gangapada said, "I am not feeling weak anymore — they have pumped a lot of blood into me." He laughed out aloud.

"Then begin your story."

There was a glass of water on the table next to his bed — he lifted himself up on one elbow and drank some water. Then with a smile he began his story with a smile.

"My name is not Gangapada Choudhury — it is Ashoke Maiti. How I became Gangapada after coming to Calcutta is a strange story.

I live in Meerat. My forefathers had settled there even before the Sepoy Mutiny. So I have very little connection with Bengal.

I do a small job in Meerat. I live with my widowed mother and an unmarried sister. I had married but my wife had died about five years ago — I did not remarry. I am trying to get a good boy for my sister.

Whatever it is — a month's leave was due to me from the office. So I thought that I would visit Calcutta. I have no friends or relatives in Calcutta. I had come to Calcutta when I was very young — then I never visited the city again. I thought to myself that I would see my homeland and also try to get a bridegroom for my sister.

I got down at Howrah station. I had got the address of a *dharmashala* from Meerat — so I thought that I would put up there. After getting down from the train I started moving towards the gate of the station. I suddenly noticed that a bearded man was walking by my side and constantly turning his head and looking at me. I felt that he wanted to tell me something. I wondered who he was — maybe an agent from a hotel, I thought.

When I reached the dharmashala, I was in trouble. There were no vacant rooms there. Now I would have to look for a hotel. But a stay in a hotel would be expensive — how would I manage? I was wondering what to do when that bearded man approached me. He was now wearing dark glasses. He said, "You didn't get a place?"

"No, who are you?"

He said, "My name is Gangapada Choudhury. Where are you coming from?"

I said, "From Meerat. My name is Ashoke Maiti. Are you the agent of a hotel?"

He said, "No, I had seen you at Howrah station — I was amazed — I will tell you why I was amazed later. Now tell me, do you have no place to stay in Calcutta?"

I said, "Why would I look for a room in a dharmashala, if I had anyone here. I can't afford to stay in a hotel. So I am thinking what to do."

Gangapada said, "I have a proposal. I live in Calcutta. My house is in South Calcutta. I am going out of the city for a month. The house will be vacant. If you stay in my house it will be convenient for both you and me. I have a part-time servant — he will look after you — you will have no problem."

I was surprised, "You will hand over your house to a totally unknown person!"

Gangapada smiled and said, "In that case I will tell you why I was amazed to see you at the station. You look very much like my younger brother Durgapada. Durgapada is missing for the last two years — probably he has become an ascetic. You bear an amazing resemblance to him. So I have developed a soft spot for you. Besides if you stay in my house, I will also be relieved because it is dangerous to lock up a house and go for a holiday nowadays."

I considered myself very lucky. I agreed very happily.

Gangapada took me to his house in a taxi. It was a small room on the first floor in a small lane. There was a bed with bedclothes, a few shelves against the wall, a few boxes and cases and that's all.

The Hindi-speaking part-time servant was present — his name was Ramchatur. Gangapada gave him money to bring tea and snacks from a shop. After the servant left Gangapada opened the window overlooking the lane outside, and came back to sit on the bed. He said, "Sit down, I have something more to tell you."

I sat down on the bed too. Gangapada said, "My landlord stays in Kashipur — he is not a nice man. If he gets to know that I have kept a man in my house for a month and have left Calcutta — he may create trouble. So if anyone asks your name — you say that you are Gangapada Choudhury. People will think that I have shaved off my beard. They will not doubt anything because we resemble each other."

I found it amusing. I said, "That is no problem at all."

Then Ramchatur came with tea and snacks. Gangapada was very kind and hospitable and said, "I will go now. You stay here without worrying about anything. Good bye."

He went to the door and came back to me again, "I haven't said something to you. When you are at home please look out of the window sometimes. Please watch out for a man with a red coat. If you see him please note down the date and time. Alright?"

"O.K."

Gangapada went away. I thought that the man was an eccentric. But whatever it was — he was a good man. I was quite comfortable in his room. Ramchatur was there to look after me. I roamed around here and there. I stayed at home during noon and night. Occasionally, I looked out of the window for a man in a red coat. But it seemed impossible that any man would walk about the streets of Calcutta in a red coat. But since I promised Gangapada — I did this duty. He could be right.

I spent a week in comfort.

This morning I went to the newspaper office to put in a matrimonial advertisement for my sister. After returning, I rested a little after lunch. Ramchatur left after he finished his work.

I got up from my afternoon nap at about a quarter to three. I opened the window and looked out. Suddenly I felt a terrible pain in my head — I fell down on the floor. Then I cannot remember anything.

I regained my consciousness in the hospital. Now I am lying with a turban tied on my head. It seems that someone had shot at my head and missed it. What is the matter, Byomkeshbabu?"

"It will take some time to get to the bottom of this mystery. You can rest now." Byomkesh got up to leave.

At about ten thirty in the morning next day, Rakhalbabu came to Byomkesh's house. He was going through advertisements in the newspaper lazily in his office chamber. He offered a cigarette to Rakhalbabu and said, "Anything new?"

Rakhalbabu lit a cigarette and said, "Ramchatur is absconding."

"Oh, that servant?"

"Yes, after informing the police yesterday, he has gone into hiding. We just can't trace him."

"True to his name — he is very clever. He doesn't want to get involved with the police. By now he has probably reached his village in Bihar and is enjoying roasted maize — any other news?"

"We informed the landlord in Kashipur. We brought him to the hospital. His first reaction was that the patient was Gangapada Choudhury himself. When he heard his voice, he said that it was someone else but the resemblance was amazing."

Byomkesh repeated, "Is there a great resemblance between Gangapada Choudhury and Ashoke Maiti?"

Rakhalbabu said, "Gangapada had said that Ashoke resembled his brother — so there could be a resemblance between these two."

"I think Gangapada's beard was false."

"I think so, too. But it is difficult to understand his motive. Why did he bring Ashoke to his house? Why did he bequeath his name to Ashoke? It is difficult to understand."

Byomkesh stopped himself from saying something, then said in a lazy voice, "It is puzzling. Gangapada is still missing, I presume?"

"Yes. We got some papers from his shelf and found out from those that he works in an iron factory and has gone on leave for a month."

"Where was the bullet fired from?"

"From the opposite house — there is an abandoned house on the opposite side of the lane. Someone had shot at Ashoke from the window of that house. We found some fresh fingerprints on the window of that house, which directly faces the window of Gangapada's house. But it is difficult to identify the fingerprints."

Byomkesh put aside the papers and asked, "Has the mystery become a little clearer?"

Rakhalbabu puffed at his cigarette and said slowly, "The fact that Gangapada's beard is false is quite obvious. His landlord had never seen Gangapada with a beard. I had asked him that. Now the question is why does he move about in disguise. One reason may be that he wants to commit a terrible crime and does not wish to be identified. He saw Ashoke Maiti in Howrah station, found that he looked like him, so he brought him to his house, and went into hiding. Maybe he himself tried to kill Ashoke Maiti from the opposite house — to try to convince people that it was Gangapada who was dead. Maybe he wanted to get a large amount from the Life Insurance Company. Now the situation is that we neither know who he is nor his present address, nor do we know for a certainty whether he really tried to kill Ashoke Maiti. There was no Life Insurance Policy among his papers. So what to do now?"

Byomkesh thought for a while, then said, "Have you made enquiries in Meerat?" "I have made Ashoke send a telegram to his mother in Meerat — we haven't got a reply as yet. Why, do you suspect Ashoke?"

"Ashoke seems a good man but he has no alibis. Maybe he is telling the truth. Ramchatur could have verified what Ashoke is saying — but he has run away. Anyway, where does Gangapada work?"

"In an Iron Foundry near Calcutta," Rakhalbabu brought out a notebook from his pocket and read out — "Scrap Iron and Steel Factory Ltd."

"We may get some information there."

"I am going there — will you come with us?"

"Yes. I have nothing to do at home at present."

The factory was in the southern outskirts of Calcutta. It was situated on two acres of land. There were some sheds here and there with corrugated roofs, between these were piles of rusted iron rods. The busy activity in the factory showed that it was a flourishing one. At one side of the gate was a small concrete house — this was the office of the factory.

When Byomkesh and Rakhalbabu reached the factory, the owner, Ratanlal Kapadia was in the office.

Kapadia had been living in Bengal for the last three generations, so he could speak fluently in Bengali although he was a Marwari. He offered us cigarettes and asked us what he could do for us.

Rakhalbabu glanced at Byomkesh and began asking his questions — Byomkesh listened quietly.

"Does Gangapada Choudhury work here?"

"Yes, he is at present on leave."

"What work does he do?"

"He is a melter in the Electric furnace."

"What is that?"

"Nowadays iron is melted in Electric furnaces — the man who knows how to do that work is a melter. Gangapada is our senior melter — it has become inconvenient for us because his assistants are not too good at the job now that he is on leave. There are very few good melters in our country — Gangapada is one of them."

"Really? Why did he take leave?"

"A month's leave was due — he has gone for a tour of India. Nowadays there are many special trains which take people on a tour of the whole of India at reduced fares."

"Yes. Does he have relatives?"

"I don't think so. He lived alone."

"What kind of a person is he?"

"Very active, good at his work, intelligent and alert."

Rakhalbabu looked at Byomkesh, Byomkesh was listening a little inattentively — now he asked, "Does Gangapada have any enemies?"

Ratanlal frowned, "Enemy? No I haven't heard of any enemies — but, oh!"

He suddenly laughed, "Yes, Gangapada did have an enemy but he is in jail at present."

"Who is he?"

"His name is Naresh Mandal. He was our chief melter for three years, Gangapada was his assistant. There was some quarrel between the two. Naresh was a hot-tempered man and Gangapada was cunning. But both were efficient. I used to watch the fun. Then one day suddenly Naresh killed a man. Gangapada gave a testimony in the court against him. Naresh was sent to the prison."

"Do you know the duration of his sentence?"

"I don't know exactly — maybe four or five years. After Naresh went to jail, Gangapada became the chief melter," he laughed heartily.

Byomkesh stood up smilingly, "We won't bother you anymore — just one thing, when did you last see Gangapada?"

"About fifteen or sixteen days back."

"Did he have a beard then?"

"Beard? He never had a beard."

"Thank you!"

Rakhalbabu asked after coming out into the street, "Now what?'

Byomkesh said, "The only thing left to do is to grope around in the dark. We can do another thing. Naresh Mandal went to jail after committing a murder about four or five years back. It might be helpful if you can get copies of all the court documents. At least if we can get a copy of the Magistrate's verdict — it would be useful. We may even get some clues from it."

Rakhal said, "All right — since I have nothing better to do — I will do that — you will get all the information by tomorrow."

The next day, Byomkesh was looking out of the window of his own house. He noticed children wearing red dresses, women wearing red sarees but not a single male wearing a red coat. A man wearing a red coat was indeed an unusual and rare sight.

The telephone rang at that moment. Rakhalbabu said, "I received a copy of the verdict of the case. There doesn't seem to be anything important — anyway I am sending it to you through a bearer — you can read through it."

A constable delivered the document to Byomkesh after about half an hour. It was a heavy official document running into fifteen or sixteen pages. Byomkesh started reading the document after lighting a cigarette.

Before giving the verdict, the Judge had given a description of the incident which led to the crime, then there was an account of what the witnesses had to say, then came the verdict. This was the summary of the whole case:

"The accused is Naresh Mandal, Age 39. He works in a factory called, "Scrap Iron and Steel Factory Ltd." He is accused of killing a street beggar. The case has been set up according to Penal Code 304/323.

We learn from the primary witness Gangapada Choudhury and other witnesses that the accused is ill-tempered and quarrelsome. At five o'clock, on the day of the crime, the accused Naresh Mandal and witness Gangapada Choudhury were returning from their work place, together. Both work in the same, abovementioned factory. Gangapada Choudhury is the assistant of Naresh Mandal.

While walking through the market place, Naresh picked a quarrel unnecessarily with Gangapada. So Gangapada allowed Naresh to walk ahead of him. He was walking about twenty yards behind Naresh.

At that time an Anglo-Indian beggar wearing pants and coat started following Naresh, asking for alms. The beggar was thin and pale but he spoke in English. He was a well-known figure in the market place.

Gangapada noticed while walking behind Naresh that he was waving his hands irritably to get rid of the beggar but the beggar was very insistent.

Suddenly Naresh lost his temper and gave a hard slap to the beggar. The man fell on the street but Naresh did not even wait to see what had happened to him and walked off angrily.

Gangapada had witnessed the whole incident. He came forward quickly and found that the beggar was dead. The post mortem report said that the man was physically weak, so a hard blow was enough to kill him.

In the meantime, many other spectators had collected around the man. Many had seen Naresh slapping that man. They informed the police. The police arrested him from his house.

According to the police, those who were witness to the case were objective about the whole incident except Gangapada. The accused had pleaded not guilty. According to him Gangapada is his enemy, he wants to take his place in the factory by removing him, that was why he had framed Naresh in this case.

It is true that Gangapada was not selfless or objective as far as this case was concerned but his statement was similar to the other eyewitnesses of the case. So Gangapada was not lying.

So Naresh Mandal has been accused of committing a murder unwillingly. According to Section 304 of the Penal

Code he is condemned to three years of rigorous imprisonment."

Byomkesh finished reading the document. It was evening and the room was dark. Byomkesh sat silently for a long time and then got up to switch on the light. Then he picked up the telephone.

"Rakhal, I read the document."

"Did you understand anything?"

"I got the analysis of the character of an ill-tempered man."

"So it was no use reading the verdict."

"I won't say that — it is better to investigate every angle of the case to get a clue."

"That's true."

"Did you take photographs of the fingerprints which you got in the abandoned house?"

"Yes."

"Did you get any news of Gangapada?"

"No, we even checked the names of passengers in the tourist special trains."

"Maybe he didn't even go — he is hiding in Calcutta."

"Maybe — any other news?"

"We have just received a telegram from Meerat. Ashoke Maiti is not lying."

"Good, anything else?"

"No, now what should we do?"

"I can't think of anything else. Can you find out when Naresh Mandal will be released from jail?"

"I will give you this news tomorrow."

About nine in the morning, Rakhalbabu came to Byomkesh. He looked grim. He said, "The matter is serious. Naresh Mandal had come out of the jail a month and a half back. He had been given a few months remission for good behaviour."

Byomkesh said, "Where has he gone after being released from jail?"

"He did not go to his old quarter, neither did he go to the factory. So he is untraceable."

Byomkesh was silent for some time and said, "Things are becoming clearer now. Naresh must be guilty of plotting some crime or else why should he go into hiding? He should have gone to Kapadia's factory to get back his job."

"I think so too."

"We can now organise the story in its correct order. Naresh Mandal was ill-tempered and quarrelsome and Gangapada Choudhury was cunning. They worked in the same factory. The two often quarreled with each other. Gangapada wanted to oust Naresh and get his position in the factory. But that was not possible because Naresh was a good worker. Then all of a sudden, Gangapada got his opportunity. Naresh hit a beggar in the street and killed him. That was a great chance for Gangapada. He tried his best to get Naresh hanged.

But Naresh did not get a death sentence, in fact he didn't even get a life sentence. He was jailed only for three years. Gangapada became the chief melter in his place in the factory.

Naresh was not only bad-tempered, he was revengeful also. Before going to the jail, he had made a vow that he would kill Gangapada, once he was out. This hatred increased while he was in jail and his resolve grew stronger.

Gangapada knew that Naresh was in prison for three years only — so he was on his guard. When Naresh came out a few months before his term was over, Gangapada was aware of the fact. He was frightened. He may have seen Naresh moving around near his house or in the abandoned house opposite his window. He decided that he would vanish from sight for a month at least.

He took a month's leave from the factory, got hold of a false beard and began roaming around in it so that Naresh would not be able to recognise him. Maybe he was really intending to go on a tour of India, before he saw Ashoke Maiti in the Howrah station one day. Strangely, Ashoke looked very much like him.

Gangapada was a very cunning man. He made a plan. He would install Ashoke Maiti in his house. Naresh would mistake Ashoke for Gangapada and kill him. Gangapada would be safe although he would lose the job — but his life was naturally more important than his job. Gangapada was sure that Naresh would kill him from the house opposite his window.

Now let's consider Naresh's point of view. Naresh had somehow managed to acquire a revolver after getting out of the jail. He did not get back to his old home, he lived elsewhere and he began moving around Gangapada's house for an opportunity. He thought that he would kill Gangapada inside his own house from the abandoned house across the lane. That would attract less attention than if he shot at him in a public place. After that he would escape from Calcutta.

In the meantime, Gangapada set up poor Ashoke in his house and went missing. Before going he told Ashoke to look out of the window for a man in a red coat. That of course, was total nonsense. His main purpose was to make Ashoke Maiti look out of the window — so that he would be a sitting target for Naresh.

Everything went off as planned, except that Ashoke was only injured and did not die. He told the police everything. Now Gangapada and Naresh were in the same boat. None of them could appear in public. Both were wanted by the police.

Naresh, of course, was a criminal, he could be caught for attempted murder. But Gangapada was no less a criminal — he had pushed an innocent man towards sure death. But even if he is caught it would be difficult to punish him."

Byomkesh became silent. Rakhalbabu said, "That may be — but how to catch the person who can be punished by law — that is Naresh Mondol?"

After remaining silent for some time, Byomkesh said, "The only way to catch him is to advertise."

"Advertise?"

"Yes, to wait for the fish to bite the bait."

After three days, an advertisement appeared in two major dailies in Calcutta:

Bombay Steel Foundry Ltd.

We require an experienced melter for our Bombay Factory.

Salary – 1000 – 75 – 3000.

Come for an interview in the address given below between 10 am to 5 pm with certificates." Just above the

Gariahat Market, there was a signboard hanging over a small room — "Bombay Steel Foundry Ltd. (Branch Office)"

Inside the room, Rakhalbabu was sitting at a table in plain clothes, attentively looking at some papers. A little away from him Byomkesh sat at a small table with a typewriter. There was a uniformed bearer at the door. Others were around but invisible to the common public.

The first day Byomkesh and Rakhalbabu sat in the office between 10 am. to 5 pm. No one came for a job. While locking the room, Rakhal said, "We must continue putting the advertisement in the papers."

The next day a man appeared. He was lean and thin. It seemed unlikely that he could kill anyone with one blow. His name was Prafulla Dey — an electrician. He had never worked as a melter. He could learn the work and do the job if he was given the chance. Rakhalbabu got rid of him.

On the third day another man came into the room. Rakhalbabu became alert as soon as he saw him. He was strongly built, dark complexioned, his eyes were blood shot, he had a crew cut and he was wearing a khaki coat. He looked askance at them, as he entered the room. He stood in front of Rakhalbabu's table and said in a hoarse voice, "I have come here after seeing the advertisement."

"Sit down."

He sat carefully on the chair opposite and looked at Byomkesh with sharp eyes. Rakhalbabu said in a very normal voice, "Have you come for the job of an electric melter?"

"Yes."

"Where are your certificates?"

The man was silent for sometime. Then he said, "I have lost my certificates. I was ill for three years and I had to leave my job. Then I lost my certificates."

"Where did you work earlier?"

"In an Iron Foundry in Nagpur. Look, I really know the work of an electric melter. If you don't believe me, I am ready to go to Bombay at my own expenses and prove this fact."

Rakhalbabu looked at the man and said, "That's not a bad proposal. But this is only a branch office. We have just opened it. I cannot take this decision on my own. I will inform my head office in Bombay. Please come tomorrow at this time."

"Certainly I will come."

Rakhalbabu looked at Byomkesh, "Bakshi, take down his name and address."

Byomkesh said, "Yes, Sir."

The man hesitated a bit before giving his name and address. Then said, "My name is Nrisinha Mullick. Address is 17, Kunja Mistri lane."

Byomkesh took down his name and address. In the meantime Rakhalbabu pressed a bell hidden under his table, which alerted the police outside that they must follow this man. Rakhalbabu was sure that this was Naresh Mondol. But before he could be arrested one needed to know the address of his house where the revolver could be found.

But nothing was necessary!

Naresh was about to step out of the door, when another man entered the room. There was no doubt that this was Gangapada Choudhury. He looked like the twin brother of Ashoke Maiti. He was without a beard this day.

Before Gangapada saw Naresh — Naresh had seen him. He roared like a lion and pounced on Gangapada. He clutched at his throat, abused him profusely and said, "Today I will not let you go, you swine."

Rakhalbabu quickly blew his whistle. All the constables and policemen around the building came running into the room. With great effort, the two were separated. Naresh was handcuffed, Rakhalbabu said, "Naresh Mondol, I am arresting you on the charge of trying to murder Gangapada Choudhury."

But Naresh was quite oblivious of anything else except his hatred for Gangapada, "I will kill you, treacherous fox."

Byomkesh sat comfortably on his chair and lit a cigarette.

Rakhalbabu told his assistant, "Dhiren, this is Naresh Mondol's address. Search his house, I am sure you will get the revolver with which he tried to kill Ashoke Maiti. I am taking these two to the lock-up."

Gangapada was sitting on the floor, trying to recover from Naresh's sudden attack. He got up quickly and said, "Why should you take me to the lock-up? What have I done?"

Rakhalbabu said, "You tried to get Ashoke Maiti murdered. The public prosecutor will decide under which penal code your crime will be tried. Get up now."

In the evening, Rakhalbabu and Byomkesh were sipping tea in Byomkesh's house. Rakhalbabu said, "How did you guess that both would come to the office for a job?"

Byomkesh said, "It was a possibility. But I really did not expect them both to arrive at the same time and start fighting like this. But it was good that we caught two fishes with one bait. Did you get the revolver in Naresh's house?"

"Yes, the case against him is strong. Now let's see if we can catch Gangapada. I have kept him in custody. Let's see what happens. At least it will be some kind of retribution for his wickedness."

"What about Ashoke Maiti?"

"He is still in the hospital. But even when he comes out, he will be our main witness — so he cannot leave the city."

Byomkesh laughed, "Thank God he is alive. If he had died — this mystery would never have been solved."

The Phantom Client
(Shailarahasya)

Shayahadri Hotel,
Mahabaleshwar,
Pune

3rd January

Dear Ajit,

I couldn't write to you after coming to Bombay. You know how difficult I find to write letters. You are a writer so you are capable of writing long letters. But where will I get your imagination? I only deal with truth!

Still, I am sitting to write this long letter to you. You will understand why I am undertaking this Herculean task, as soon as you come to the end of this letter. I am writing this letter in candlelight from the hotel room of Mahabaleshwar, a hill station. It is cold and dark outside. I am sitting in a closed room but I am unable still to avoid the cold and the dark. The wick of the candle is flickering. There are long shadows moving silently on the walls. Indeed, a ghostly atmosphere! I have always tried to avoid dealing with the supernatural in my life — but — it is becoming difficult for me to keep it out of my business here. As I am unable to relate a story as you do, I have first written what I should have related later -— I must begin from the very beginning!

I took about four days to finish my work in Bombay. I had decided to return on the same day. But I had got acquainted with a police bigwig — Mr. Vishu Vinayak Apte — Maharashtrian. He said, " How can you go back from Bombay without seeing Poona?"

I asked, "What is there to see in Poona?"

He said, "Poona was the Great Shivaji's capital. There is lots to see there — Singh Garh, Bhabani Mandir, etc."

I thought that I might not come to this part of India again — so why miss the chance of seeing places.

I said, "Alright, I am interested."

We started out in Apte's car. The road from Bombay to Poona is beautiful. It weaved in and out of the Shayahadri Mountain Ranges of the Western Ghats. It is difficult for a person like me to describe the scenic beauty of these parts — on one side are the mountain ranges, on the other — deep gorges. You would have written an epic on the beauty of this place.

I was a guest in Apte's house in Poona. There was no dearth of hospitality. Poona is colder than Bombay. But this cold does not make one feel numb, instead one feels energetic.

I stayed in Poona for three days and saw all that had to be seen. Then Apte said, "How can you leave Poona without seeing Mahabaleshwar?"

I said, "What's that?"

Apte laughed and said, "It's a place. It is the best hill station of Maharastra — just as your Darjeeling. It's two thousand feet higher than Poona. Everyone from Bombay goes for a holiday in Mahabaleshwar during the summers."

"But no one goes during the winters. How cold is it?"

"It's like the weather in England — let's go — you will like it."

So here I am in Mahabaleshwar — and am I enjoying myself.

Mahabaleshwar is seventy-five miles from Poona. We started out by car after lunch and reached Mahabaleshwar at about four in the afternoon. On reaching we found that the town was virtually empty, except for a few permanent residents. It was really "home" weather here — as Englishmen would say — severe cold during day, severe cold during night. I had borrowed a heavy overcoat from Apte — or else it would have been impossible for me to bear the cold. The town was a smaller version of Darjeeling. Apte and I put up in the Shayahadri Hotel. There was not one guest in the hotel. Only the owner of the hotel was there with two or three servants.

The owner is a Parsi gentleman called Shorab Homji. He is an old friend of Apte — middle-aged, plump — very fair. He must be a good businessman but he is also a very amiable person.

Apte introduced me to him — he looked at me sharply — then welcomed me to his sitting room — coffee and pastries came soon after. The sun had set by the time we had finished our coffee. Apte went out to meet a relative of his who lived here. He said that he would return within an hour.

After he left, Homji smiled and said, "You are a Bengali. You will be surprised to know that a month and a half back this hotel belonged to a Bengali couple.."

I was surprised, "What are you saying? A Bengali came and started a hotel so far away!"

Homji said, "But he did not start it alone, he had a Gujarati partner."

The servant came and said something to Homji. He asked me, "Hot water is ready, do you want to have a bath?"

I said, "Are you crazy? In this cold! I will bathe only after returning to Bombay."

Homji laughed. I asked him, "Your home is in Bombay — then why are you staying here in this cold. There are no beaches here now."

Homji said, "There is a lot of work to be done here. Visitors will start coming from March. So the hotel has to be painted and tidied up by then. Then I have made a rose garden at the back of the hotel. Why don't you come along with me, it is still daylight — I am sure that you would like to see the garden."

The garden was at the back of the hotel. Flowers will begin blooming in a month or two. The hotel was a white-washed, two storeyed house. It had about twelve to fourteen rooms. A red pathway passed the front of the house. At the back, after the rose garden, was a deep gorge. If one bends down — one would notice a dense forest and a stream, deep down in the gorge.

We were returning indoors when a roar echoed in the gorge. By now it was pitch dark below. I asked, "What was that?" Homji said, "A tiger's roar. Let's go in." The electric lights were on inside — the servant brought a coal stove near us. We pulled our chairs near it. I asked, "So there are tigers here?" Homji said, "Yes, there are also cheetahs, hyenas and wolves. The tiger which you heard roaring is unable to leave the place because he has tasted human blood."

"It is a man-eater — how many humans did it kill?"

"I know only of one. It is a very exciting story — do you want to hear it?"

Just at that time, Apte came back — the exciting story was forgotten. He said that his relative had requested him to have dinner and spend the night in his house— so Apte would go there for the night and return at nine the next morning to take me to the places of tourist interest over here — Bombay Point, Arther's Seat, Pratap Ghar Fort etc. He went off. We chatted for some time. Then suddenly Homji asked me, "I hope you are not afraid of ghosts."

I laughed. Homji said, "Some people are afraid to sleep alone. Then shall I make arrangements for you to sleep in the first floor?"

I said, "Most certainly. Where do you sleep?" he said, "I sleep downstairs. My bedroom is next to my sitting room. I am asking you to sleep in the first floor because we have put away all the bedding in the storerooms as there are no visitors. Only one room on the first floor is ready. The previous owner stayed in it with his wife. We have not moved anything as yet from that room."

I said, "No problem, I will sleep there."

We had our dinner at eight in the evening. It seemed like midnight — everything was dark and quiet. I asked Homji, "You did not tell me your exciting story."

Homji said, "Yes, indeed, it is an exciting story. This incident has to do with the two previous owners of this hotel." Homji began his story.

About six years back, a Gujarati named Manek Mehta and a Bengali named Bijoy Biswas started this hotel in Mahabaleshwar. They were equal partners. Mehta gave the money, Bijoy Biswas, the hard work. And the hotel started.

Manek Mehta had a lot of other work and was hardly ever in Mahabaleshwar. He only came occasionally. Bijoy Biswas was the person who ran the hotel, with the help of his wife, Haimabati.

Manek Mehta was not a good man. He had three wives, one in Goa, one in Bombay and the other in Ahmedabad. He lived in one or the other of these places. He had many illegal businesses, too — he was a bootlegger, a smuggler and what not. Many a times, his goods had been confiscated but he was never caught. He was as slippery as an eel. No one knew how Bijoy Biswas and Mehta met and decided to start a hotel business — because Biswas was not that kind of a person. As far as common knowledge goes Biswas was experienced in the running of hotels. He had a small hotel in either Bombay or Ahmedabad. The kind of business that Mehta was involved in brought him a lot of money sometimes and sometimes not a penny. So he had decided to invest in a hotel for rainy days. Biswas probably did not know what kind of a man he was, so he trusted Mehta and partnered him in this business.

With the good management of Biswas and his wife, the Shayahadri hotel became one of the best in Mahabaleshwar. Here the tourist season is only for two-and-a-half months — or a maximum of three months. The couple worked so hard that within a few years the profit of the hotel doubled. Mehta came at the end of the tourist season to collect his part of the profit.

During these years, Shorab Homji, was a regular visitor to this hotel during the summers. He liked this hotel and dreamed of owning one himself someday.

The previous year, Homji came to stay as usual in May. As an old client he was given a lot of importance. Haimabati took special care to make him comfortable. One day she told Homji sadly, "Sethji, next year you will not see us here."

"Why?"

Haimabati said, "The hotel will be sold. Our partner is not willing to keep the hotel anymore. We will also leave and return to our own state. My husband does not keep well in this cold climate."

That evening, Homji met Bijoy Biswas in his office, "Are you thinking of selling the hotel?"

Bijoy Biswas was about forty-five years of age — much older than his wife. He looked a little sickly. He always wore a lot of warm clothes including a muffler, even during the summer.

He said, "Yes? Do you want to buy it?"

Homji said, "Yes — if the price suits me. But where is your partner?"

"My partner is abroad now — he has given me the power of attorney to sell the place." He opened his cupboard and showed Homji the document.

Finally, after a lot of bargaining the place was sold to
Homji. But the whole process of registration took a few
months. In the middle of November, Homji and Biswas
went to Poona and in the Registrar's office, Homji paid the
money in cash. It was decided that he would take possession
of the hotel on the 1st of December. After that Homji went
to Bombay and Biswas returned to Mahabaleshwar from
Poona.

There were no guests in the hotel at that time. There was
only a maid there. So whatever happened after this was
known only from Haimabati's testimony. Manek Mehta
must have given the power of attorney to Biswas purposely,
because the very next day after the transaction, he arrived
at the hotel at 9 p.m. Later it was found out that Manek had
left his car two miles away from Mahabaleshwar and had
walked all the way to the hotel.

When he arrived at the hotel, Biswas and his wife were
planning what they were going to do in the future. They
had finished their dinner. The maid had gone off to sleep.
It was quite cold then. Mehta was wearing a heavy overcoat
and a woollen monkey cap. His behaviour was always
perfect. He said, "Haimaben, I will eat and stay here tonight.
Make me something simple."

Haimabati went to the kitchen to make something for
Mehta — she did not wake up the servant. Mehta and
Biswas began talking about money matters. There was a
strong iron locker in the office, all the money from the sale
of the hotel as well as some of the money from the bank
was kept there. Biswas knew that Mehta would arrive any
day to take his share.

Although Haimabati was cooking, her ears were alert to any conversation in the office room. She heard two men come out of the office room and go out of the house, to the back garden. She was very surprised — because Biswas could not tolerate the cold, winter air. But still she could not imagine that anything untoward was about to happen. She continued cooking.

Then she heard a faint scream from behind the house. She was terrified. That was her husband's voice! She ran to the back of the house through a door opening on the back yard. As soon as she opened the door, Mehta rushed in. He pushed Haimabati aside and ran towards the front door.

"What's wrong? What's wrong?" screamed Haimabati and ran out into the back yard. There was no one there. She then ran into the office room — she found the iron safe wide open and all the money missing. Now she realised that Mehta had pushed her husband into the gorge and escaped with all the money. She screamed and fainted.

Dear Ajit — I will have to stop here. The disembodied soul has started disturbing me! I will finish my letter tomorrow.

4th January

I could not finish my letter yesterday, I have started writing again today in candle light, after 10 p.m. Homji was telling me the story. We finished having our food before he finished relating the story. We came back to the sitting room. The servant served us coffee. Homji began speaking :—

When Haimabati regained her senses it was past ten — the lights had gone off. She called her maid but there was no one to help for that night. The police came the next morning. Police investigation showed that Haimabati was correct. There were signs of struggle at the back garden at the edge of the gorge. More information came to the police gradually. Manek Mehta was absconding. He was smuggling three lakhs of gold from Pakistan, when the Customs department confiscated the goods. He gave the police the slip but had become penniless. So he had murdered his partner and had vanished with all the money from the safe.

It was necessary to retrieve the body of Bijoy Biswas from the gorge. But this gorge was so inaccessible that it was a very difficult task to go down in search of the body. Moreover, a tiger couple had come to live in the valley below the gorge. One could hear them roar in the night. Anyway, the police went down the gorge with a few tribals — into the valley, in search of the body. But they found very little of the remains of the body. They came up with a few bones, some blood-stained clothes and a muffler — all belonging to Bijoy Biswas. The police issued an arrest warrant against Mehta.

It was soon the 1st of December. One could easily imagine the condition of the poor, destitute, widow. Homji was a kind man, he gave some money to Haimabati. She left Mahabaleshwar for good, wiping her tears of grief and loss.

A month passed. Manek Mehta was still absconding. But the tiger and the tigress were still living in the gorge. They had tasted human blood and so were unable to leave the place.

I was a bit sad when I heard Homji's story. I felt sorry for a fellow Bengali who had made some money but had lost all of it and also his life. But the condition of his widow was of course, worse. I wondered if the police would ever be able to catch Manek Mehta. It was a difficult job in a country like ours, where the population was vast.

I was thinking about all this, when the lights went off. Homji said, "Here lights go off at ten at night and come back early in the morning. Come, let me see you to your room."

He had a huge, long torch with which he showed me the way to my bedroom. There was a row of rooms, all of them were locked except the last room in the corner. There was a long verandah in front of the rooms. The servant had kept a candle on the table.

The room was big, in front was the verandah, and at the side, a balcony. There were two single beds on either side of the room. One was made, the other bare. In the middle of the room was a large table and two chairs. There was a wardrobe against the wall, an alarm clock on the table, a box of candles, a box of matchsticks and a flask full of coffee — in case I felt cold at night. Homji was indeed hospitable.

Homji said, "Bijoy Biswas lived here with his wife. This room has not been used after Haimabati left. I hope you will be all right."

I said, "I will be very comfortable — don't worry. You go and rest. I think it is usual for people to retire early in this place."

Homji smiled, "Yes, especially in the winters. No one stirs before eight or nine in the morning. If you want to get up early, you can put on the alarm. Keep this torch, you may need it at night."

"Thank you."

Homji went downstairs. I closed the door. In the light of the candle, shadows were playing in the room. My suitcase was kept next to the wardrobe. I sat on a chair and lit a cigarette.

Although all the doors and windows were shut, chilling cold air filled the room. I quickly smoked my cigarette and put the alarm at seven thirty in the morning. Apte will come at nine.

I kept the torch next to my pillow, put off the candle and slipped under two comfortable and warm blankets. I dozed off to sleep. I received no hint of the presence of the supernatural till then.

Suddenly I was rudely woken up by the sound of the alarm clock. I sat up — was it seven thirty already? I flashed the torch on my watch — it was two o'clock and the clock on the table too indicated two. Did I make a mistake in putting on the hands of the alarm at the right time? The clock must be a defective one. I went off to sleep and got up the next morning.

This was my first night's experience. At breakfast the next morning, I asked Homji, "Is there something wrong with the alarm of the clock in my room?"

He said, "No, why?"

I told him. He looked worried. Then he said, "Maybe it has stopped. I will give you another one tonight."

At that moment the servant came in with Apte's letter. He had written that the previous night he had sprained his ankle in his relative's house — he could not move his legs — could we please come to meet him.

I asked, "How far is it?"

Homji said, "Apte's relative is the manager of a bank, situated in the market place about two miles away. The manager stays on the top floor of the bank."

We drove down in Homji's car. We climbed the stairs of a two storeyed house to reach the first floor. We found Apte lying in bed with his feet on a pillow. He was happy to see us, "Just look at my condition I should have been showing you round the place but here I am in bed."

I asked, "What happened?"

Apte said, "I heard someone knocking at my door at night and jumped up from bed. I opened the door and found no one. So I shut it again and as I was walking towards my bed, I fell down and sprained my left ankle."

"Have you hurt yourself anywhere else?"

"No, but —" Apte was quiet for sometime, "Strangely, I didn't trip and fall. I felt as if I was pushed from behind."

I suddenly asked, "What was the time then?"

"Exactly two."

We did not speak about it any more — the host had come to welcome us. He was a jolly man. We had coffee and snacks and chatted for some time. Apte said, "I thought I would take Mr. Bakshi around but I will not be able to move for two or three days."

Homji said, "Don't worry, I will take him around. I am free now."

We went back to the hotel after promising to come back the next day. Homji took me out after lunch to see a few famous spots.

After coming back, I asked Homji for a letter pad which is nearly finished now. That night I went to bed five minutes before ten. The servant had kept everything in order. I noticed that he had also kept a new alarm clock instead of the old one. I did not wind the alarm but locked the key. I did not need an alarm — I would get up whenever I wanted to.

Suddenly I noticed a big black moth flying around the room. I was thinking if I should open the door to let it out, when the lights went off.

I was lying in bed and thinking. The alarm rang at two at night and two miles away Apte sprained his ankle. It must have been a coincidence. But if he had not sprained his ankle — he would have been sleeping in this room, on the other bed.

I had dozed off when I woke up with a start. The new alarm clock was ringing. But I had not wound the alarm, in fact I had locked the key!

I got up from bed and flashed the torch — it was two o'clock at night. The key of the alarm clock was locked but still the bell was ringing. What was wrong? I got up from bed and took the clock in my hands — the sound stopped.

Ajit, you know that I don't like any mysteries. If I encounter anything mysterious — I want to get to the bottom of it. But what was the mystery here? My practical attitude is against anything supernatural — this was something I could not prove. But what was this? These happenings could not be explained by any reasoning.

I really have to find the truth. I lit a candle. I had already written to you that there were two chairs in the room — one was an ordinary chair and the other a rocking chair. I sat on the rocking chair, lit a cigarette and began rocking gently.

I was facing the door. On my right was the table, on my left the wardrobe, and behind me was the bed. The moth began flying again.

I was thinking, with my eyes closed. Both the alarm clocks began ringing at two in the night — was this Homji's practical joke on me? He did not seem that kind of a person — but I did laugh yesterday when he asked me about ghosts. I will examine the clock myself. But Homji was an elderly man, would he crack this kind of joke? It seemed unlikely.

I don't know for how long I sat rocking the chair — not more than ten or fifteen minutes at the most — suddenly I opened my eyes and found that I was facing the wardrobe and not the door. Not only that, I had come quite close to the wardrobe.

The chair could turn for natural reasons. But if a thing like this happened at two at night — your senses do receive a jolt. Then suddenly the alarm clock started ringing again. I jumped up to stop it — suddenly the candle flickered and went off.

If my nerves had been weak, I don't know what I would have done. I stiffened my body and forced myself to be calm. I lit the candle again — took up the clock and it stopped ringing.

But this time I kept the clock inside my clothes in the wardrobe — so that even if the alarm went off — the sound would be muffled. There was a strange smell of camphor and perfume inside the wardrobe. I shut the door and lay down in bed.

I could not sleep well — suddenly I felt something moving inside the blanket near my chest. I threw away the blanket, lit the candle and found that the black moth had somehow made its way inside the blanket. It was now half-dead. It was three-thirty at night, by my watch.

I sat for the rest of the night on the other chair. This letter is becoming too long. I will finish it quickly. At five in the morning, the lights came on again. I took out the clock from the wardrobe. A slip of brown paper came out with the clock, with an address written on it. The address was written in Bengali. It was that of a locality in the southern end of Calcutta. I am sending the address to you — you will need it.

Then I opened the inside of the watch with my penknife and found that there was no defect in it.

This time I had to admit the truth — because I am a truth seeker — even if the truth was a supernatural one! I addressed the disembodied spirit in the room, "What do you want?"

There was no answer, but the table moved — I had my hand on the table. I said, "Do you want me to investigate your murder?"

This time not only did the table move but even two legs of the chair went up — I nearly fell on the table.

I said, "But the police is investigating — what will I do? Where will I start investigating?"

Suddenly the slip of the brown paper with the address, which was on the table, flew towards me.

Then I thought, is Manek Mehta hiding near Calcutta? Maybe — is he alone or —?

I said, "Alright, I will try."

I saw the light of dawn slowly coming in through the window.

I did not say anything to Homji. We went to see Apte at nine in the morning. On the way I asked Homji, "What did Haimabati look like?"

Homji smiled at me, "Very attractive — not very fair — but attractive."

"Age?"

"A little above thirty, maybe. But she still looked young."

Apte was a bit better, but not completely well. We met his relative. I asked him, "Did you know Bijoy Biswas?"

"Yes, he had deposited all the money of the hotel in my bank."

"Did he have personal account?"

"Yes, but he had withdrawn most of the money a few days before his death — only a few hundreds are left. However his wife cannot withdraw it unless she gives a succession certificate — that will take some time."

"Do you know Haimabati's present address?"

"No."

"Does anyone here know?"

Homji replied, "I don't think so, because she herself was not sure where she would be going, poor soul."

I asked Apte, "You must be knowing about this case. Have the police found out the whereabouts of Manek Mehta?"

He said, "No. I would have heard about it otherwise."

"Is there any photograph of Manek Mehta?"

"There was a group photograph of Manek, Bijoy and Haimabati, when they started the hotel. But it is missing."

I slept soundly after returning to the hotel. I started writing to you at night but could not complete my letter after being disturbed repeatedly. Anyway I am completing my letter today.

You must have realised by now what I want you to do. You will please go to this address in the southern part of Calcutta. If you don't meet Haimabati Biswas there, then there is nothing else to do. But if you meet her, then ask her these questions. Where is the group photograph which she and her husband took with Manek Mehta? Try to guess how close she was to Manek Mehta. Where did Mehta first meet the Biswas' and when? What is the financial condition of Haimabati at present? Who are there with her now in the house? Moreover, ask her any other question which you would want to. Then write back to me in detail — don't leave out anything even if you feel it is not important. If you find anything suspicious — send me a telegram immediately.

I will wait for your reply. I don't feel like staying on here in this cold. But I am unable to leave without solving this case.

With love,
Byomkesh.

Calcutta,

8th January

Dear Byomkesh,

I received your letter this morning and I am writing to you at night. My dear agnostic, isn't it a shame for you to fall into the clutches of a ghost!

Anyway, according to your instructions, I was getting ready to go out about three in the afternoon when Bikash Dutta (our assistant) arrived. When I told him where I was going, he exclaimed, "Goodness, that's at the back of beyond, will you be able to find the address on your own?"

I said, "Then why don't you accompany me?"

He agreed, but I did not give him the details of the case.

The place was really far. When we reached our destination, I found that there was one straight road and the houses were few and far between. We reached the address given by you at about four thirty. As it is the winter is severe this year — even in Calcutta it is quite cold in the evenings. Here we found that it was quite cold even at four thirty in the afternoon, probably because of the open space all around.

The small one-storeyed house was a little distance away from the road and it was surrounded by fields. There were no houses nearby.

I told Bikash, "You wait outside the house, I may return immediately or after an hour."

I knocked at the door. After quite a while, a servant opened the door and said, "Who do you want?"

I said, "I want to meet Haimabati Biswas."

He asked, "What is your name?"

I said, "Ajit Banerjee."

"What do you want to see her for?"

"I will tell her that. Just inform her that I have come with a letter from Mahabaleshwar."

"Please wait," said the servant and shut the door. I stood outside for about ten minutes. Then the door opened again and the servant said, "Come in."

There were two chairs and a table in the small room. The servant said, "My mistress is taking a bath, please sit down."

"How long have you been working here?"

He said, "About a month."

I noticed that he spoke with a strong east Bengali accent.

"Where is your original home?"

"Faridpur, in East Bengal."

He sat down on the ground. He was middle-aged and was wearing a dirty, torn sweater.

"How many years have you been in Calcutta?"

"About three years."

"How many people stay in this house?"

"The mistress stays alone."

"She is a woman — she stays alone in this lonely place?"

"I am an old man — I look after her — she is very good to me."

"Does she have visitors?'

"No, sir, you are the first visitor I have seen since I started working here."

At this point, Haimabati appeared at the door. She told the servant, "Mahesh, bring a lantern."

It was getting dark outside. Even in the faded light, she looked beautiful and dignified. She was fair and attractive. She was wearing the white saree of a widow, and no ornaments. I know you will tease me for my poetic description of the lady — but she looked like a stalk of rajanigandha — wet in the evening mist. Her long wet hair was left open.

I greeted her and she returned the greetings.

She asked, "Are you coming from Mahabaleshwar?"

I said, "No, my friend Byomkesh Bakshi, the Truth Seeker, is in Mahabaleshwar — I have come to meet you after I received a letter from him."

This time there was an eagerness in her voice, "Has Manek Mehta been traced?"

"No, not yet."

Haimabati sat on a chair slowly and said in a disappointed voice, "Why have you come to me?"

"My friend, Byomkesh Bakshi" I began.

"Is he in the police department?"

I eagerly gave all your details with pride and here I would like to tell you that you are not as famous as you think you are. This lady did not know of your existence, she was quite indifferent.

"I don't know him, I have always lived away from Bengal."

The servant brought the lighted lantern and put it on the table.

In the light of the lamp, I saw her face clearly. It was a beautiful face but with a tired and disappointed expression. A few strands of wet hair crowned her face. I felt ashamed to harass this grief-stricken lady.

I said, "Please forgive me, Byomkesh has told me to ask you a few questions in connection with the arrest of Mehta. When did you first meet him?"

Haimabati said, "Six years ago. We had a small hotel in Ahmedabad. It was our bad luck that we had come across a man like him."

"Were you close to Mehta?"

"I had personally met him about five or six times. He came only twice every year. He came stealthily to collect the money and left in the same way."

"Did you not suspect him for this?"

"No, we thought that it was his nature."

"Do you have any photograph of him?"

"There was a group photo in the office room of the hotel but on that fateful night — when I regained consciousness I found that the photograph was missing."

"How much money was there in the hotel safe that night."

"I am not sure — but a few lakhs."

Then I did not know what else to ask and was preparing to leave — when she asked, "How did your friend know my address? I haven't given it to anyone."

Naturally, I could not broach the topic of ghosts in her present state of mind, so I said, "I am not sure. Will you be here now?"

She said, "I think so. A friend of my husband took pity on my condition and allowed me to stay in this house."

I found that it was quite dark outside when I came out of the house.

Bikash was waiting for me. We luckily got an empty taxi and boarded it.

Bikash asked, "Did you get your work done?"

"Yes, somewhat." I was not certain myself. Bikash was quiet for some time. Then he said, "When you write to Byomkesh babu tell him that there are two beds in the bedroom."

"How did you know?"

Bikash said, "When you were talking to the lady — I peeped into all the windows of the house."

"What else did you see?"

"I saw an iron safe in the bedroom — the servant was trying to open it."

"Are you sure you saw the servant?"

"Yes, the same man who opened the door for you. There is no other male in the house."

We reached home quite late. Bikash has just left. Now I am sitting down to write to you."

Yours affectionately,
Ajit.

I am Ajit Banerjee — writing the rest of the story. My letter was posted to Byomkesh in Mahabaleshwar on the 9th of January. At about three in the afternoon of the 12th, Byomkesh arrived in Calcutta.

I was surprised, "What is this? Did you get my letter?"

"As soon as I got your letter, I took a plane. Get ready fast, we have to go out immediately." He went into his office.

Within half an hour we went out of the house and found a police van waiting for us with an inspector and a few constables. We got into the van.

After some time, we reached Haimabati's house. But now no one came to open the door for us — it was already open. We entered the house and found it completely empty, except for the furniture. The door of the safe was open but there was nothing inside.

Byomkesh smiled helplessly, "The birds have flown."

After dinner that night, we were relaxing in our sitting room. Although all the doors and windows were shut — the cold, winter wind was making its way into the room.

I said, "I think you have brought some of the cold from Mahabaleshwar. I hope you haven't brought Bijoy Biswas's ghost, as well."

Byomkesh looked at me smilingly, "Your wrong idea about the ghost is still there."

I said, "Naturally, I have never seen a ghost — so how will I have a right idea about one? Tell me Byomkesh, is it possible that you have started believing in ghosts?"

"Do you believe in the existence of Byomkesh Bakshi?"

"Of course, I can see him sitting in front of me."

"If I say that I felt the presence of the spirit — what will you say to that?'

I was quiet. Then I said, "We won't argue. But tell me, in spite of all the efforts of your ghost — the mystery remains unsolved."

"Who told you that the mystery has remained unsolved? The spirit wanted us to see through a great deception — it was successful in doing so."

"What does that mean?"

"Have you not understood anything?"

"Of course, I understood. At first I misunderstood Haimabati. Now I know that Haimabati and Manek Mehta were in love and together they killed Bijoy Biswas. She is a terrible woman."

Byomkesh laughed. He said, "I want to ask you a few questions, Ajit. Why did Manek Mehta take Bijoy Biswas near the gorge to murder him? Why did Bijoy Biswas go with him?"

I thought for some time and said, "I don't know."

"My second question to you is — why did Bijoy Biswas withdraw nearly all his money from his account in the bank in Mahabaleshwar?"

I shook my head.

"My third question is — when you went to meet Haimabati — it was a cold, winter evening. But the servant told you that she was having a bath — did you not find it strange?"

"It did not strike me as strange."

"My fourth question, did you not suspect the servant?"

"Why should I — he was employed only a month back. But of course if he was stealing from the iron safe in the bedroom..."

"Ajit, your simplicity is really touching! True, the servant was trying to open the safe — but not to steal. In Mahabaleshwar two people plotted to kill a person. One was Haimabati — who was the other one?"

"Who else but Manek Mehta?"

Byomkesh said with a meaningful smile, "That is the great deception. Haimabati plotted the murder with her husband, Bijoy Biswas and not with Manek Mehta."

I was stunned, "What are you saying?"

Byomkesh said, "When Homji told me the story — I was not very impressed. But I found one thing a bit strange. Why should Manek Mehta take Bijoy near the gorge to kill him?

Then my phantom client began pestering me. I had to start investigating. I found an address written in Bengali, in a slip of brown paper in the wardrobe — things were becoming slightly clear to me then.

I wrote a long letter to you. When I received your reply, I was quite sure that I had come to the right conclusion. I told Apte everything. He rang up the police in Calcutta and arranged for me to return by plane.

Although we couldn't catch Haimabati and Bijoy Biswas — the spirit's wish was fulfilled. We got to know who the true culprits are. Who knows, one day they may be caught, now that the police are on the right track. It was Manek Mehta's insistent spirit which made me take up the case."

"What really happened that night?"

Byomkesh said, "No one knows what really happened except Bijoy and Haimabati. I have only come to a conclusion through assumptions.

Manek Mehta was a terrible crook but Bijoy was a hypocrite. One day the two met and opened a hotel. Mehta gave the money and the Biswas couple put in their hard work.

The hotel was doing well. The yearly turnout was good. Mehta came sometimes to collect his share. Bijoy Biswas did not keep much money in his account in Mahabaleshwar — probably he kept it in his wife's name in a bank in Calcutta.

Everything was all right, suddenly Mehta got into trouble — his smuggled gold was confiscated. He escaped but became bankrupt. The only asset, which he had, was the hotel. He decided to sell the hotel. He needed cash.

Now the question was, who would get the money out of the sale of the hotel? It is my assumption that since Manek Mehta gave the money for setting up the hotel, it was likely that he would claim the whole amount. I think that is what he did.

But Biswas and his wife decided that they would take all the money. We don't know the history of the couple but I am sure they too had a criminal background. It was easy to put all the blame on Mehta as he was a known criminal. The couple planned the murder to its minutest detail.

They had rented the house in Calcutta through some agent — Haimabati wrote the address and put it into her wardrobe. But by the time she left, she knew the address by heart so she forgot to take the slip of paper. That was a grave mistake she made.

Anyway, Mehta arrived that night as quietly as he usually came. There were no guests in the hotel. The maid went off to sleep. The only people in the hotel were Biswas and Haimabati.

I think they killed Manek Mehta in the office itself — in such a way that there would be no bloodshed. Then Bijoy Biswas dressed Manek in his own coat and muffler. They carried the body to the back garden and pushed it into the gorge. The tiger couple, which had been living in the gorge, devoured the body and left the blood-stained clothes and a few bones for the police to investigate and identify.

Bijoy Biswas escaped with all the money, no one saw him in the dead of the night. Haimabati stayed back. Everyone knows what happened after that. Manek Mehta was blamed for the murder, as he was known for his criminal activities.

So Haimabati came to live in the house in Calcutta, Bijoy accompanied her there. But they were very careful. You were made to wait until Haimabati dressed like a widow — why else should she wash her hair in that cold winter evening, obviously to wash off the vermilion in the parting of her hair.

Anyway, when Haimabati entered the room — Ajit, you were struck by her freshly bathed, innocent beauty. You mentioned my name to her. My dear Ajit, don't think that I am not as famous as I assume. As soon as she heard my name, she became alert. Bikash had seen two beds in the bedroom and the servant trying the lock of the safe. These two pieces of information cleared all my doubts. I came rushing back. But unfortunately the culprits could not be caught. As I said earlier, now that the police are on the right track, thanks to the efforts of my disembodied client, they may be caught one day."

I said, "But Byomkesh, why didn't Bijoy Biswas stay in that house? Where did he stay? Didn't the servant suspect them for their strange behaviour?"

Byomkesh sighed exasperatedly, "Dear God, Ajit, did you understand nothing? That servant was Bijoy Biswas."

Quicksand
(Chorabali)

We, that is Byomkesh and I, Ajit, could not ignore any longer the repeated requests of Kumar Tridib to visit his estate. So one cold December morning we left Calcutta for a break of seven or eight days. Our intention was to relax completely for those days, and return bright and fresh for work again, to Calcutta.

There was no dearth of hospitality. We spent the first day just snacking every hour and chatting non-stop with Kumar Tridib. The main topic of our discussion was, of course, Kumar Tridib's uncle, Sir Digindra, mentioned in the story — Hidden Heirloom.

After dinner, Tridib ushered us to our bedroom and said, "We will go out early tomorrow morning for hunting. I have made all the arrangements."

Byomkesh asked enthusiastically, "What kind of game do you find?"

Tridib said, 'Not tigers but rabbits, wild boar, deer, peacocks, wild ducks — there is a large jungle at the border of my estate. The jungle belongs to Himangshu Roy — the zaminder of the adjoining estate called Chorabali, quicksand. Himangshu is a good friend of mine. I informed him this morning about our visit, and also asked his permission to hunt in his area. I hope you don't mind?'

We both said together, "Mind?"

Byomkesh added, "Only there are no tigers — that's disappointing."

Tridib said, "I can't say there are no tigers. Every year one or two tigers do visit this area, but don't depend on it. Besides, even if a tiger is available, my friend Himangshu will bag it — he won't allow us to hunt it." He began laughing. "He has no time to look after his estate — he is so addicted to hunting. He spends most of his time either in the room where he keeps his guns, — or he is roaming around in the forest. He is crazy about hunting. His aim is also remarkable. He can shoot a tiger standing on the ground."

Byomkesh said curiously, "What did you say was the name of the estate — Chorabali'? Strange name!"

"Yes, we have heard that there is a patch of quick sand somewhere in the jungle. But no one knows where exactly it is. That is why this strange name was given," he looked at his watch and said, "You'd better go to bed — or you'll not be able to get up early." He smothered a yawn and left.

We were given one large room with two beds. We snuggled under comfortable, soft and warm quilts, and prepared for a good night's sleep.

Soon we were fast asleep. Suddenly I found myself drowning in quicksand. Byomkesh was standing at the edge of the quicksand, watching me and laughing. Soon I was neck-deep in sand, and was gradually getting suffocated. For a moment I got the taste of a terrible death. I woke up sweating profusely — the quilt had covered my nose — hence the feeling of suffocation! I sat up on my bed for some time thinking amusedly, how our thought process could strangely filter into our sleep....

Very early in the morning there was a big rush to go out for hunting. We wore shorts and warm hoses — breakfasted on hot scalding tea and cakes and climbed into the vehicles. The car was loaded with three shot-guns, lots of bullets and a huge basket of foodstuff. Tridib, Byomkesh and I piled on to the back seat of the car and the car started at once. We sped through a cold, misty dawn. Kumar mumbled through his raised overcoat collar, "If we don't reach before sunrise, it will be difficult to get peacocks and woodcocks. At this time, they sit on the branches of trees — and are very good targets."

Soon dawn broke. There were rice fields on either side of the road — some corn sheafs were standing, while others had been cut and kept in bunches. We could see a dark green shadow in the horizon. Kumar pointed to it and said, "That is where we are going to hunt."

After about twenty minutes, our car reached the edge of the forest. We got down enthusiastically with loaded guns. Kumar Tridib went to one side. Byomkesh and I walked to the other side of the forest. This was the first time that I was going to use a gun, so I was nervous to venture out alone. Tridib and we decided before parting that we would meet at an open space on the eastern edge of the forest at about 9 a.m., when we would have our breakfast.

It was a huge forest. A variety of tall trees covered the sky. The sunlight filtered through their leaves. There was a huge amount of game available — deer, rabbits, birds of many kinds. I cannot express the great excitement which we felt when we pulled the trigger and found birds dropping dead at our feet — I could write an epic on it, but I don't want to be the laughing stock of veteran tiger hunters!

I considered myself to be equal to the legendary Arjun in aim. But Byomkesh had only used his gun twice and killed a rabbit and a peacock — he was looking for larger game — like deer, boar or even a tiger.

But as the sun rose, the fresh forest air stoked our appetites. So we began walking towards the eastern edge of the forest. We found that Kumar Tridib was also walking towards the open space.

We reached the clear space. In front of it was a large sandy patch — shaped like a half-moon. It was about a quarter of a mile in width, but we could not make out how long it was — it bordered the forest. The sunlight shone on the sand — it was a beautiful sight. This area prevented the forest from expanding eastwards. Maybe many years ago it had been a huge river, now with natural calamities and changes it had become a dry sandy area.

We sat at the edge of this huge stretch of sand, and lit our cigarettes.

Soon Kumar Tridib joined us. "I am feeling very hungry — there Duryodhan has laid out our breakfast — let's go."

We noticed that Tridib's cook was laying the food on a white sheet under a tree. We reached the spot quickly. We began talking about our hunting spree. I was chastened to find that Kumar Tridib had won hands down!

We had our fill and gulped down hot tea from a flask. Sated, we lit cigarettes and began smoking. Tridib relaxed against a tree and said, "This stretch of sand is responsible for the name of this estate. This side of the sandy area belongs to Himangshu. My area begins from the opposite edge."

Byomkesh said, "How long is this stretch of sand? Does it encircle the whole forest?"

"No. It is about three miles long — then my fields start. In between this stretch, is an area of quicksand — but no one knows exactly where it is. No one walks over the sand for fear that they may be sucked in. Strangely, even cows, foxes and dogs avoid walking on the sandy stretch."

Byomkesh asked, "Is there any water in this sandy area?"

Kumar shook his head uncertainly. "I don't know. I have heard that there is water over some area on that side — but it is not always available." He pointed towards the southern stretch which curved and vanished into the forest.

Just at that time there was a gunshot very close to us in the forest. We sat up, startled. All three of us were there with our guns — then who was shooting? Suddenly, a person with a gun in one hand and a dead rabbit in the other, came out of the forest. He was wearing jodhpuris and a boy scout cap, and a line of bullets hung from the broad belt of his breeches.

Kumar Tridib laughed aloud, "Hello, Himangshu, please join us."

Himangshubabu joined us. He said, "I should have been the one to welcome you — especially these new guests of yours." Tridib introduced us and then gently mocked him. "So you could not resist the temptation of a hunting expedition, could you? Or were you afraid that we might bag all your tigers?"

Himangshubabu said, "I am in great trouble. I was supposed to leave for Tripura today on an invitation for a hunting expedition. But I could not go. Dewanji stopped me from going. He belongs to the time of my father. So he stops me from going hunting on any excuse. I can't even disregard his wishes. So, I got out early this morning to show my ire — I can hunt a wild boar or two at least!"

Tridib teased him, "Poor you — what a fall! — a wild boar or two in place of tigers of Tripura! But why couldn't you go?"

Himangshu pulled the basket of food towards himself, and took out a cutlet and a couple of boiled eggs and bit into the food happily. I began observing him. He was about our age — and strongly built. A ferocious moustache had made his gentle face unnecessarily hard. He had the sharp and alert eyes of a hunter. At a first glance, he looked cruel and hard, but seeing him now, at his relaxed best, I felt his external appearance was not the only clue to his nature. He was a simple, unsophisticated person, uncomplicated, and a little disinterested and absent-minded about materialistic things, like the running of an estate.

While sipping a cup of tea, Himangshu said, "What did you say? Why couldn't I go to Tripura? For a useless reason.

But Dewanji is very worried, and even the police have been informed. So I have to be stuck here for who knows how many days now!" His voice was full of impatient irritation.

"What has happened?"

"What else? You know that after my father's death there have been court cases with the tenants of my estate for the last five years. The tenants were not paying their rents regularly — so there is constant unrest in the estate, constant consultation with lawyers — you know all that. In the meantime another problem has cropped up. A few months back I had appointed a house tutor for my daughter, Baby. He vanished day before yesterday. It seems he has even taken a few account books with him. That is why there is great uproar in my house. Dewanji feels that it is a great plot hatched by the troublesome tenants of the estate."

Byomkesh said, "Has the tutor not been found?"

Sadly, Himangshu shook his head, "No, and until he is found ..." Suddenly his face lit up — he looked at Byomkesh and said, "Great God, I had forgotten that you are a famous detective. (here, interrupting him softly, Byomkesh said, 'Truth Seeker!') It is your job to catch thieves and robbers. Please help us to find the tutor within two or three days, then I can still join the hunting expedition in Tripura. If I can go by tomorrow or the day after..."

We laughed aloud. Kumar Tridib said, "Can you think of nothing but hunting?"

Byomkesh said, "I don't have to do anything, the police will catch him. It is difficult to vanish totally from a small place like this — it is not a big city like Calcutta."

Himangshu shook his head, "No, the police can do nothing. They have tried their best in these last three days.

They have appointed people to watch out in all the railway stations nearby. But nothing has come out of their efforts so far. Please Byomkeshbabu, I request you to take up the case. It is a small matter — you won't even take two hours to solve it."

Byomkesh smiled at his eagerness and said, "Relate the whole incident to me in detail."

Himangshu said, "Do you think I know the details? I hadn't even met him for three days before he vanished. Anyway, I am telling you the little I know. A few days back — maybe about two months ago, an eccentric young man came to meet me one morning. I had never seen him before. He was not from this area. He was wearing a torn kurta and a torn pair of slippers. He was thin and short, and looked as if he had not eaten for a few days. But when he spoke, I realised that he was educated. He asked me to give him a job — he was in dire straits of poverty. I asked him, 'What job can you do?' He pulled out his B.Sc. degree certificate from his pocket and said, 'I'll do whatever you ask me to do.' I felt a bit sorry for the young chap. What work could I give him — there was no vacancy in the office of my estate. Suddenly I remembered that my wife had asked me for a private tutor for Baby. She is seven years old — so we would have to pay a little more attention to her studies.

"Thus he was appointed as a tutor for Baby. I found out that though he was poor, he was educated, and came from a good background. I made arrangements for him to stay in a room in the outhouse. The fellow wept with gratitude. Who would have thought at that time ... name? As far as I remember, his name was Harinath Choudhary.

"Anyway, he stayed in the house. But I hardly met him. I heard that he was teaching Baby in the morning and in the evening. Suddenly, the other day, I heard that the boy had vanished without telling anyone. I didn't mind his vanishing at all — but then I heard that he had vanished with a few account books. But because he took them with him, all my plans have been shattered. Now I won't be released from this place until he is found."

Himangshu stopped speaking. Byomkesh was lying on the grass while listening. He asked, "Where did he have his meals?"

Himangshu said, "He used to eat in the house. My wife used to give him special attention as he was Baby's tutor."

Suddenly we heard a flapping sound on the trees. We looked up to see a huge wood-cock flying from one branch of a tree to another. The gap between the two trees was about thirty feet. In a minute, Himangshu fired from his gun; the bird could not reach the other tree, but dropped dead midway in its flight.

I exclaimed, "What a crack shot you are!"

Byomkesh also said, "Really remarkable!"

Kumar Tridib said, "This is nothing. He can do much more than this. Himangshu — show them your great trick of hitting the target only by hearing the sound."

"No, no. Let's go into the forest again for another hunting spree."

"No, you have to show us your special talent … tie a hanky over your eyes."

Himangshu was embarrassed, "just look at him — it's a silly trick — you must have seen it so many times."

We too began insisting, "You have to show us."

"All right, All right… It is nothing but hitting a target merely by listening to the sound. Byomkeshbabu, tie my eyes so that I am unable to see, but keep my ears free — so that I can hear."

Byomkesh tied his eyes securely. Then Kumar Tridib took a cup and tied a string to its handle. He tiptoed to a tree twenty-five feet away and tied the cup to a branch.

Byomkesh said, "Now listen, Himangshubabu."

Tridib made a small sound with a spoon on the hanging cup. Himangshu turned the way from which the sound had come and said, "Please make the sound once more." Kumar Tridib repeated the sound and quickly walked away. Before the echo of the sound could die down completely, we heard the bullet being fired. We looked around to find that only the handle of the cup was hanging from the tree — the pieces of the rest of the cup were lying around.

We were astounded. Himangshu untied the hanky and said, "Are you happy?" He was a little embarrassed with all our praises.

Indeed it seemed like magic to us. He said, "Please stop — I am blushing … get up, let us go into the forest again."

At about one thirty in the afternoon, we returned to where our car was parked. In the meantime, the incident of Harinath's theft of the account books was forgotten. Himangshu did not show much interest now about Byomkesh taking up the case. Maybe he thought that the police would be able to solve such a simple case. But it was Byomkesh who broached the subject again. "We couldn't hear the entire story about your Harinath tutor."

Himangshu said, "I have told you everything I know, I don't think there is much more to tell you."

Byomkesh did not say anything more. Tridib said, "Himangshu, get into our car — we'll drop you home. You must have walked to the forest in the morning?"

"Yes, I crossed the field. It is much longer if I walk along the road," Tridib said, "It is about two miles along the road. Come, we will drop you home, and if you ask us to stay for lunch we will be very happy," he teased.

We did not mind going anywhere since we had come for a holiday; we were ready to humour our host.

Himangshu said, "Of course! Of course! You are my guests. I should have thought about it earlier. I am sorry for my omission. Anyway, you can rest in my house after lunch and then return home after tea in the evening."

Byomkesh said, "And if possible, try to find out where your tutor has run away!"

"Yes, that's a good idea. My Dewan may be able to give you much more information about him."

We got into the car. Although Himangshu had invited us to his house very cordially — I don't know why I felt that he was not too happy to take us all to his house.

After about ten minutes, our car entered the huge compound of his palatial house. At the sound of the car, an elderly person came out onto the verandah, and as soon as he saw Himangshu, he said in a distressed tone, "Himangshu, my worst fears have come true! Harinath not only stole the account books, but also six thousand rupees from the cash-box."

It was three in the afternoon — the mild winter sun was giving way to evening.

"I would like to hear everything from your Dewan, — Bhattacharjeebabu," Byomkesh said while reclining on some cushions.

We were relaxing together after a heavy lunch. Sitting next to Byomkesh, little Baby was dressing up her doll. The two had become very good friends in these two hours. Dewan Kaligati Bhattacharjee sat straight in a yogic *asana* — it looked as if he would start meditating if he got the slightest chance.

One could associate only prayers and meditation with a man like Kaligati. In fact, I mistook him at first for the family priest. He looked like an ascetic. He was lean and thin and very fair. He had a red *tika* on his forehead, and wore a string of *Rudraksha* round his neck. But it was he who was managing the huge property of this hunting-obsessed, impractical zamindar. Kaligati was managing every little detail of this household — from entertaining guests to money matters of the estate. Everything was running with clockwork precision because of him.

He stirred when Byomkesh spoke. He closed his eyes for some time, then said slowly, "Harinath was such an ordinary and insignificant human being that when one starts talking about him, it seems that there is nothing to say. He looked simple, but that he was so wicked seems unimaginable. I am a good judge of character — but this boy hoodwinked even me. I never suspected that this was his disguise — he had come here with other intentions.

"The first day he came here he looked so poverty-stricken that I gave him two dhotis, two vests, two kurtas and two blankets from the store-room. Himangshu had already given him a room to stay — there were old account books on the shelves of that room — otherwise it was not used. We moved a bed into that room. It was decided that Baby would study there in the morning and in the afternoon. I had decided that he would have his food with some other workers, like Anadi Sarkar, in their house — I was about to make these arrangements — when Baby's mother requested me to make arrangements for him in the house itself. So that was done.

"Then he began teaching Baby regularly. I noticed that he taught well. He used to sit with me some times and listen to the scriptures. In this way two months went by.

"Last Saturday, I went home just after evening — you must have seen the house I stay in — the yellow house on the right side as you enter the gate. I had sent my wife to my village a few months back. So I stay alone and I cook my own food — I don't mind it at all. I do a special *puja* on Saturday night — so I went home quickly to prepare for it. It was very late in the night when I finished my *puja*.

"The next morning I heard that Harinath could not be found. Soon it was twelve noon — still there was no sign of the man. I became suspicious. I went into his room and found that he had not slept on his bed the previous night. Then I opened the cupboard where the account books are kept — the books of the last four years were missing.

"For the last four years we have been fighting court cases with many of our important tenants. I felt that it must be their plot. Harinath must have been their spy. He came disguised as a tutor to steal these account books.

"I informed the police. I did not know till then that six thousand rupees were missing from the locker."

Dewanji stopped for some time and then said hesitantly, "For various reasons there was a dearth of money in our estate for the past few years. There were the expenses for the court cases too. So we had borrowed six thousand rupees from the money-lenders to tide over these problems. I had kept the money in the locker tied in a piece of cloth — it was in one corner of the locker — I have often opened the locker, but never thought of opening the bundle of cloth to check the money. Today, the lawyer asked for money, so when I unfolded the cloth I got some old newspapers instead of the money."

The Dewan was silent. Byomkesh was lying on his back, staring at the ceiling. He said, "Was the lock on the box secure — who has the keys to the locker?"

Dewan said, "The locker has two keys. One is with me and the other is with Himangshu. I have my key but Himangshu has misplaced his, and it could not be traced for the last few days."

Himangshu said with a guilty expression, "It is my fault. I can never look after my keys. I always forget where I have kept them. This time too, I could not find the keys for the last few days. I was not too worried, I thought I would get them somewhere, some day, as always."

Byomkesh sat up and pulled Baby on his lap, "Our Baby's teacher was a great one! But it is strange that he can't be found. Are efforts being made to find him?"

Dewan Kaligati said, "We are trying our best. Police are doing their work; moreover, I, too, have appointed some people. But we have yet got no news of the man as yet."

Baby threw away her doll and hugged Byomkesh, "When will my teacher come back?"

Byomkesh shook his head, "I don't know, dear, maybe never."

Baby began crying. Byomkesh asked, "Did you like your teacher?"

Baby nodded her head, "Yes, I love him very much. He taught me arithmetic — tell me — nine sevens are how much?"

Byomkesh said, "I don't know — sixty-four?"

Baby laughed, "You don't know anything — sixty-three. Do you know how to chant the hymn to goddess Kali?"

Byomkesh said helplessly, "No, my dear, I don't even know that."

Baby began chanting the hymn — when Kaligati stopped her with a smile, and sent her outside to play. After she left he said, "He was a good teacher."

Byomkesh stood up. "Let's go and see the room in which he stayed."

The room was at the end of a long verandah. The door was locked. Dewanji opened the lock with a key from a bunch tucked in his waist. We entered the room.

The room was small in size. There were two wooden cupboards, a table, chairs and a bed inside, which left hardly any space to move. Opposite the door was a small window, — Byomkesh pushed it open. Then he looked around the room. The bedclothes on the bed were neatly folded. The table was covered with a fine layer of dust. In one corner of the room, some clothes were hanging from a clothes line. The door of a cupboard was ajar. There was a picture of goddess Kali on the wall — showing the teacher's special reverence for this deity.

Byomkesh bent down and pulled out a pair of shoes from under the bed and said, "This shoe is a new one. You must have bought it for him?"

Kaligati said, "Yes."

"Strange, strange," Byomkesh kept the shoes and went upto the clothes. He lifted the washed and the unwashed clothes and said, "Strange, very strange."

Himangshu asked curiously, "What has happened?" Byomkesh was about to reply, then his eyes fell on a small shelf on the opposite side. He went towards it quickly and pulling out something, asked in surprise, "Did the tutor wear spectacles?"

Kaligati said, "I forget to tell you that — yes. Has he left his glasses behind?"

Byomkesh looked through the glasses, handed them to me and said, "Isn't it strange?"

Kaligati frowned thoughtfully, "It is really strange, because a person who has bad eyesight would never leave his glasses behind. What do you think is the reason...?"

Byomkesh said, "There may be many reasons — he may have been cheating you — he may not have had poor eyesight at all."

In the meantime Kumar Tridib and I were trying to look through the glasses. The glasses were heavy, set on a rickety frame. We could see nothing through the spectacles.

Kumar Tridib said, "Byomkeshbabu, I don't think your assumption is correct. The spectacles are worn-out with use, and they are powerful glasses."

Byomkesh said, "I may be wrong. But the tutor may have brought someone else's old spectacles to deceive everyone — that may also be a possibility. Anyway, let us look at the cupboard."

We found rows of account books on the shelves — there were about fifty to sixty such books.

Byomkesh took one out and said, "It is quite heavy — at least six kilos. Does each book have a year's account?"

Kaligati said, "Yes."

Byomkesh turned the pages and saw that it was an account of the past year which was the fifth — the most recent ones of the last four years were stolen. Byomkesh pulled out a few more and glanced through the system of accounting. Each book was divided into two parts — one portion was the rough accounts, and the other portion was the fair, permanent one. On one side, the daily income and expenditure had been noted, on the other side there was the total daily expense. This was not the way accounts were kept in estates. But this system was convenient because one could make out the expense and income, rough and fair accounts, at one glance.

Byomkesh had taken the matter very lightly in the beginning, he considered it to be an usual case of theft. But after examining the room, I noticed, there came that strange, sharp look in his eyes. I knew that look. He had stumbled on to something serious — it was not a matter to be taken lightly. I, too, became excited.

While coming out of the room, Byomkesh asked Himangshu, "Do you want me to investigate the case?"

Himangshu hesitated for a moment, then said, "Of course, so much of money is involved — the mystery has to be solved."

Byomkesh said, "Then the two of us must stay here."

Himangshu said, "Of course, of course — that is no problem at all."

Byomkesh looked at Kumar Tridib, "If only Kumar gives his consent — can we stay here, because we are his guests."

Kumar was in two minds. He must have thought that Byomkesh wanted to earn some money by solving the case. So he said, "If it helps my friend Himangshu, to have you here then…"

Byomkesh shook his head, "I can't promise that. I may not be able to do anything. Himangshubabu, if you are not interested then tell us frankly. We have come here to have a holiday in Kumar's estate, and left our profession behind in Calcutta — so if you don't require our help, we won't be unhappy."

Kumar Tridib realised that Byomkesh had been able to read his mind. So he insisted, "No, no, you stay here and solve the case — I'll come everyday to visit you."

Himangshu nodded in agreement. So we decided to stay back in Chorabali Estate.

We went back to the sitting room and had our afternoon tea in silence. The Kumar said, "It is four thirty, Himangshu, I'll leave now. I'll come some time tomorrow." He stood up to leave.

We saw Kumar off to his car. He had made plans for us — fishing, boat-rides, and so on. So he was a little disappointed. He asked us, "How long do you think this case will take you?"

Byomkesh said, "I really can't say. You must be thinking how ungrateful I am. But, Kumar, the matter here is serious — I should not neglect it."

Kumar looked startled, "Really? I had thought it was not so serious ... of course a lot of money has been stolen —."

"The theft of the money is of secondary importance."

"Then?"

Byomkesh was quiet for some time, then he said in a grave voice, "I think Harinath is not alive."

We were both startled. Kumar said, "What are you saying?"

Byomkesh said, "I think so. I hope you will forgive me after hearing this."

Kumar said anxiously, "There is no question of forgiving you. If a man has been murdered — it our duty to find out the culprit."

Byomkesh said, "I am not saying that he has been murdered. But he is not alive. Anyway, we cannot talk about it unless we get more proof. Please come tomorrow, and bring our suitcases with you. You had better go — you will be late reaching home."

We started walking towards the house after Kumar had left. It was quite a distance between the gate and the house. There were many plants in the beautiful garden. There were benches to sit and relax.

We left the small house belonging to the Dewan to the right, and walked ahead. It was a dark winter evening, only a red streak of sunlight could be seen in the west above the heads of the trees in the forest.

Byomkesh was walking slowly with a worried expression. I could not fathom his thoughts. What did he see in the room that made him so sure of Harinath's death? I was a bit absent-minded while thinking of all this. A very serious event had occurred in this small, quiet place to upset the calm life of the people here. One can never understand the existence of a whirlpool by seeing its calm surface. Having been present with Byomkesh in many of his cases, I had realised that it was difficult to make out a person's character by looking at his exterior, so also it was difficult to gauge a situation by merely judging it superficially.

Byomkesh lit a cigarette standing under an eucalyptus tree. Then he said to himself, "The only reason for Harinath not to wear his shoes could be that shoes make a noise. But why should he not wear his kurta? Why should he leave his spectacles behind?"

I said, "But, how do you know about his kurta?"

Byomkesh said, "At the Dewan's order, he was given two kurtas, two vests from the store. He himself had brought a torn kameej. All of them were hung on the line."

I was quiet for some time, then I said, "So you surmise that...."

Byomkesh was looking at the sky — a small, curved moon could be seen on the western sky. He pointed to it and said, "Ajit, have a look, the moon is still very small — what was it like that night?"

I shook my head to express my ignorance. Byomkesh said, "It must have been a new moon night — a very dark night — let's consult the almanac." I heard a new excitement in his voice.

I had always thought that poets and romantics were excited by the moon; so I was a bit surprised at Byomkesh's enthusiasm — as I knew him to be most unromantic and unpoetic. But by now I was getting used to his unpredictable behaviour; so I followed him to the house silently.

The part of the garden which we had reached was about fifty yards from the house. If we walked straight we would have to cross a small grove of pine trees; the grove separated this part of the garden from the rest of it.

We walked silently on the grass and reached this grove, when we heard someone sobbing. We slowed down our pace automatically. I looked at Byomkesh — he had put a finger on his lips, to ask me to be quiet.

We heard a voice through the sobs, "Babu, this Anadi Sarkar has seen you grow up from a little child. Have mercy on your old servant. The mistress has misunderstood. My daughter has made a mistake — but I can vow that we did not commit that terrible sin."

There was no sound for some time — then we heard Himangshu's harsh, low voice. "Are you telling the truth ... you haven't killed?"

"Master, I promise you, we did not. If I am lying to you, my employer, then let God never forgive me."

Again there was no response for some time. Then Himangshu said, "But you can't keep Radha here any more. You send her away tomorrow — make the arrangements. If people get to know about this incident, then I will not be able to show you any mercy.... As it is, there are a lot of problems in the house."

Anadi said anxiously, "I will send her to Benares tomorrow — an aunt of her stays there."

"All right, if you can't bear the expenses..."

Byomkesh pulled me by the hand. We tiptoed away from the place.

After about fifteen minutes, we reached the house by a different, roundabout way. Kaligati was standing on the verandah, talking to a servant. Baby was pulling at his hand, and asking him to do something for her. We heard part of what she was saying, "Why don't you call out only once...."

Kaligati said in an embarrassed manner, "You crazy girl! Not now."

Baby pleaded, "Please, Dewandada, they will also hear" — she pointed towards us.

Kaligati came forward to meet us. He dismissed the servant, and asked us in a serene voice, "Were you strolling in the garden?"

Byomkesh said, "Yes ... what is Baby saying — who does she want you to call?"

Kaligati said with a helpless smile, "This girl is the limit! She wants me to imitate the call of a fox now!"

Surprised, I said, "What is that?"

Kaligati turned to Baby and said, "I am busy now, don't disturb me. Go to your mother and sit down to study."

But Baby was insistent, she held on to his finger and said, "Only once, Dada."

Kaligati whispered something into her ears, and then said loudly, "Just before you go to sleep, I will call for you — all right. Now, my dear, please go away."

"All right."

After Baby left, Kaligati told us, "My man has come back from the police station. There is no trace of Harinath."

Byomkesh said, "Oh! Tell me, is there any servant called Anadi?"

"Yes, Anadi is the head servant of the estate," Kaligati looked curious.

Byomkesh thought for some time, "I don't think I have seen him. Does he stay in the servants' quarters?"

Kaligati said, "No, he is a very old servant. Behind the house, near the stables, there are a few rooms — he stays there."

"Is he alone?"

"No, he has his wife, and a widowed daughter. His daughter has been ill for the last few days. I had asked him to take her to the doctor — but he is not agreeing — he says she will be all right. Why are you asking all this?"

"No — nothing in particular. I wanted to know which employees stay nearby. Do the other servants stay outside the compound?"

"Yes, there are seven or eight living quarters for them. It takes long for them to come to work from the town, so, my master, Himangshu's father, made this arrangement."

"How far is the town from here?"

"About five miles. The road in front goes straight east to the town."

Just then, Himangshu came out of the house. He said, smiling at us, "Come, Byomkesh and Ajitbabu, let me show you my armoury!"

We followed him eagerly. It was evening — Dewanji went off quickly to prepare for his evening prayers.

Himangshu took us to a middle-sized room. On a table at the centre of the room, a light shone. We noticed that the floor was covered with the skins of tigers, bears and deer. There were some almirahs on the wall. Himangshu opened them one by one, and showed us different types of guns, pistols, revolvers and rifles. We were a little surprised to see this man's great affection for all those terrible weapons. He described the quality of each, and even recalled which was used to kill what animal. He said that he never allowed anyone to touch these; he cleaned and oiled them himself.

After seeing the arms, we sat there in the room, and started chatting. We talked about many subjects. People reveal their characters in different ways, in different environments. The relaxed atmosphere of the room helped Himangshu to unravel himself. I was quite certain that this man was a simple person, and that his mind went in a straight direction like the bullet of his gun.

We unwittingly began talking about estates, and the problems in managing these. Himangshu told us a lot about himself and about the estate he ran. He told us frankly that he was bitter about the constant clash with his subjects. The earnings were virtually nil — court cases were costly. So in these last few years the debts were running into lakhs. I noticed that this bitterness had made him turn away from property matters. He was not very sure of the impending dangers because he was inexperienced about money matters, but he was vaguely aware of some unknown catastrophe in the near future. To divert his mind from this fear, he plunged himself into his favourite sport — hunting. Such was the present situation.

It was eight thirty in the evening; we were called for dinner. Now we saw Anadi Sarkar. He had come to call us. His eyes had a restive and anxious expression — as if he was afraid of being caught for a misdeed.

Byomkesh observed him with sharp eyes. Then we followed him to the dining room. After dinner, we were escorted to our room by Bhuban — Himangshu's personal bearer. We relaxed on chairs and lit cigarettes. Bhuban put up the mosquito curtains, placed a jug of water on the table, and was about to leave, when Byomkesh asked, "You had seen Harinath for the last six months, did he always wear his spectacles?"

Bhuban probably knew that we had come to investigate the theft — so he was very eager to speak.

"Yes, sir, he wore it all the time. One day he was going for his bath without it and he tripped and fell. He could not walk a step without his glasses."

Byomkesh said, "How many pairs of shoes did he have?"

Bhuban smiled and said, "How many — only one, Sir — that also the master had given him. The one which he had worn to this house was so torn that even a dog would not chew it. We threw away that pair into the dustbin, that very day."

"Really? Did he bring the picture of goddess Kali with him?"

"No, Sir, — he did not bring even a toothpick with him. He brought that picture from Dewanji, and hung it on his wall."

Byomkesh said, "All right, thank you."

Bhuban said, "Do you want anything else, Sir?"

"No, but can you bring me an almanac?"

Bhuban was surprised, 'Do you want it now, Sir?'

"Yes — if it is possible."

"I will bring one, Sir."

We were smoking silently while waiting for Bhuban to return, when suddenly, very close by, foxes began howling continuously. Probably five or six foxes had collected together nearby. We got over our initial shock.

Bhuban returned with the almanac. I said, "Are foxes allowed to come so close to the house?"

Bhuban controlled his smile and said, "Those are not real foxes. Babydidi was insisting that Dewanji should imitate the call of foxes. He is making that sound."

I remembered, "Yes, yes, Baby was asking Dewanji this evening. This is a great talent — it is difficult to make out that it is false."

Bhuban said, "Yes, Sir, Dewanji can imitate the calls of all the animals very well." He kept the almanac on the table, next to Byomkesh. I glanced at Byomkesh and found him sitting motionless like a statue. His eyes were staring fixedly, his muscles were taut — I asked in surprise "What's the matter?"

Byomkesh woke up from his trance and said, "Nothing — so this is the almanac. Alright Bhuban — you may go now."

Then Byomkesh began turning the pages of the book and stopped at a certain page; he pushed the book towards

me and said, "Look at this" — his voice was trembling with
excitement. I looked at the page to find out that the night
Harinath vanished had been a new moon night.

We got up at seven the next morning and found that the
whole house was asleep. We learnt from a servant who was
sweeping the verandah, that no one stirred before eight
thirty on a winter morning.

How were we to spend this hour and a half? The sun
was not out properly — there was a hint of a mist. I was
restless. I told Byomkesh, "Let's go out into the forest, and
shoot a few birds — we have nothing to do now — we'll
come back by the time these people get up."

I had just learnt to shoot, so I was very enthusiastic.
Moreover, Kumar had left the two guns we had used
yesterday, in this house — some bullets were also left in the
pockets of our coats.

Byomkesh thought for some time and said, "Let us go."

We started out with the guns on our shoulders. We
asked the servant which road we should follow. He said
that if we followed the straight road, we could walk by the
side of the stretch of sand, and enter the forest. We began
walking.

After walking for some time, we could see the trees of
the forest about a mile away. By the side of the forest was
the stretch of sand. From far it looked like a canal bordering
the end of the forest.

The direction in which we were walking was the
southern part of the stretch of sand. It had tapered off at

the southern tip to meet the forest. So there was no more sand in the southern direction.

After walking for almost fifteen minutes, we reached that southern tip. We found that there was kind of embankment there. This was about fifteen feet in width. On one side of the embankment was the stretch of sand, and on the other was the green field.

We climbed onto the embankment and looked down to see that there was a faint line of grass, after which began the sea of sand. I wondered where in this sea would be that terrible area of quicksand.

The first thing we noticed when we climbed on to the embankment was a small, dilapidated hut. It was situated at the extreme limit of the embankment from where the area of sand began. The roof was low, the walls were made of burnt mud, but much of the wall had broken off in portions. The thatched roof, too, was broken. Probably no one had lived there for the last four or five years. We were surprised to find that hut in such a lonely place so far from human habitation, and so near the forest. Byomkesh said, "Let's explore the inside of the hut."

I was just getting ready to follow Byomkesh, when I saw a flight of wild doves in the sky. Byomkesh quickly fired a shot, and one bird fell on the sandy stretch just below us. I was getting ready to climb down the embankment to retrieve it, when Byomkesh said laughingly, "Why are you so impatient? A dead bird won't fly away — let's first explore the hut."

We entered the hut and found that it had two entrances, the one through which we entered had no door, but the door at the back of the hut, which opened on the stretch of sand, was still — intact.

There was nothing usable in the room. There was an overgrowth of grass on the mud floor, some parts of the broken roof also crowded the room. It was a longish room, but the width was about six feet.

Byomkesh keenly observed the floor and said, "Someone had come here recently — see, Ajit, the grass and the broken thatch is pressed down here. Someone has pulled something across the floor here. People frequent this hut, I am sure."

I did not think it was impossible. Shepherd boys would definitely come in here for a rest, when they came with their flock. So I said absently, "Maybe," my mind was on the dead bird on the sand.

I opened the back door of the hut to look out for the bird, but saw nothing. I was sure it had fallen there. I called Byomkesh, "Where is the bird — your dead bird has really flown away!"

Byomkesh too came out of the back door and said, "Strange!"

"Maybe it has fallen just a little ahead — we can't see it from here. Let me get down from this embankment." I got ready to climb down and step on to the sand, when Byomkesh pulled me back by the collar of my coat. "Stop it!"

"What happened?" I said, surprised by the expression on his face.

"Don't step onto the sand."

He threw the empty cover of the bullet about twenty feet out into the sand. My hair stood on and end with fright at what I saw next! The cover stood up on its edge, and was sucked into the sand until there was no trace of it anywhere.

So this was the quicksand! I was about to step into it! I started trembling with nervous reaction. I looked at Byomkesh with gratitude and said, "If it was not for you, brother..." But Byomkesh was not listening to me at all — he kept on saying in a whisper, "How terrible, how terrible!" Then he broke a few pieces of wood from the roof and threw them on the sand — each of these disappeared. We could not make out the area of the quicksand; however far we might throw, the pieces kept disappearing. We came into the hut again through the back door. Byomkesh said, "Ajit, don't tell anyone that we have found the area of the quick sand. Do you understand?"

We came out of the front door of the hut and Byomkesh turned round to have a look at it.

"Have you observed the position of the hut? Behind it is the quicksand, in front of it is the forest, on either side is the embankment. I would like to know who had it made."

The mist had cleared. I looked in front to see a person in shorts with a gun on his shoulder striding out of the forest towards us. It was Himangshu. He said, "Where were you, I was looking for you inside the forest?"

Byomkesh said to me in an undertone, "Ajit, don't say a word about the quicksand." Raising his voice he said, "Ajit forced me to come out to shoot birds, but the birds are safe. Ajit has become crazy, he will soon be arrested by the police under the Arms act."

Himangshu came to us and asked, "So did you get something?"

"Nothing, but why have you come out early in the morning with your rifle?" Byomkesh asked.

Himangshu said, "I heard this morning that a tiger's roar has been heard in the forest. So I quickly came out. The servant said that you also had gone towards the forest — so I was worried. If you are confronted with a tiger, your small guns would be useless."

Byomkesh asked, "Who told you that there was a tiger in the forest?"

"No one is certain. But my milkman was saying that the cows were restless the whole night — probably they have smelt a tiger. Then Dewanji told me that he had heard something like a tiger roar from the forest. Anyway, let's go back and have tea."

Byomkesh looked at his watch and said, "Eight thirty, let's go. Tell me to whom does this small hut belong? And why was it built in this lonely spot? Do you know?"

Himangshu said, as we walked towards the house. "About four or five years back, after my father's death — a sadhu who was a worshipper of goddess Kali appeared in my house. He looked terrible. He was tall and big, his face was covered with a big beard, he had a head full of long hair, his eyes were bloodshot. He looked at me and told me that he wanted to be my guest.

"I don't like all this, and have no respect for this type of sadhus — so I was ready to turn him out. But Dewanji prevented me from doing so. He himself is a worshipper of Kali — so probably his heart flowed with reverence for this man. He began pleading with me to keep that man as my guest, to avoid being cursed. But I refused. Finally we came to an agreement. He would stay somewhere in the estate in a hut which would be made for him, while his food would be sent regularly from the house. I had to agree to this, because Dewanji was so enthusiastic.

"That sadhu chose this spot, and his hut was made here. He was here for about six months. I did not meet him any more. But Dewanji used to visit him regularly. He was even initiated by the sadhu. Dewanji was always a Kali worshipper, but now he became very devout.

"Anyway, the sadhu vanished one day as suddenly as he had come — but the hut remained."

By this time we had reached the house. We had our breakfast in the large open verandah. As we were enjoying a sumptuous breakfast, Kumar Tridib arrived with our suitcases. He asked Byomkesh, "How far?"

Byomkesh shook his head uncertainly, "Not very far — but I am expecting to find a solution in a few days' time. I want to go to the town today to get some information from the police."

Tridib said, "Very well, I'll take you in my car and come back by twelve noon."

Byomkesh shook his head, "No, I will take some time. It will be evening by the time I return. I'll have my lunch and go out."

Kumar said, "All right, that's also okay with me. Himangshu, why don't you come with us — we haven't been to the town for a long time!"

Himangshu said hesitantly, "No, I have some work — I won't be able to go today."

Byomkesh said, "No, you don't have to go. Ajit can stay back too. We both will go." He looked at Tridib — there must have been some signal in his eyes because the latter stopped himself from saying something.

At about eleven Byomkesh went out with Kumar Tridib. He told me before going, — "Keep your eyes open. Notice everything that happens in my absence."

After the car went out of the gate, I felt that on Himangshu's face there was an expression of the sheer joy of freedom. The old suspicion, that he somehow was not happy at our arrival and stay in his house, began haunting me again.

Dewan Kaligati was nearby. He was an extremely shrewd man. He might have guessed the tension between us, because he called me to the verandah and began conversing easily about various subjects. Himangshu joined us too. The main topic of our conversation was Byomkesh. I always loved advertising the talents of my friend — so I did that now quoting many examples. I also hinted that this household was lucky to get his help. Then I said, "That Harinath is not alive, could be discovered so quickly only by a person like Byomkesh."

Both were startled, "Not alive!"

I was in a fix — I did not know whether I should have revealed the fact. But Byomkesh had not asked me to keep this a secret. Still I felt that I should not have blabbered. I controlled myself and knowingly shook my head, "Everything will be revealed to you in time."

It was twelve noon, so we got up. But though neither of them asked any more questions, I could realise that both were disturbed by the news of Harinath's death.

I was thinking of spending the whole afternoon alone as Himangshu said that he had some important work. But Baby kept me company. She asked me where Byomkesh was, and apologised for not coming earlier as her cat had given birth to kittens. Then she began letting out many secrets of her family by talking continuously. She suddenly said, "My mother hasn't eaten for three days."

I asked, "Is she sick?"

She shook her head gravely, "No, she had a quarrel with my father."

I was considering whether it was civil enough to ask any more questions on this subject, when I noticed a green sedan silently going out of the gate — the driver was Himangshu himself. I could not see whether there was any one inside the car.

Baby said, "That is our new car."

I felt that Himangshu's actions were surreptitious. Where did he go? Was there any one with him? He was trying to hide something from us right from the beginning. Our arrival had put a spoke in his wheel. So he was very anxious and impatient, but could not express it. Did he know anything then about the disappearance of Harinath? Or was he shielding some one? Why was Anadi Sarkar crying yesterday? He said that he had not committed any crime — what crime? Today Baby said that her parents were having a quarrel. What were they quarrelling about? Was Harinath responsible for this quarrel?

"Can you draw pictures?" Baby asked — I came back to the present.

"Yes," I said absent-mindedly.

Baby ran out of the room and came back with an exercise book and a pencil. "Please draw a nice picture for me."

The exercise book was Baby's arithmetic book. Her name was written in an adult handwriting on the first page.

I asked. "Is this your teacher's handwriting?"

"Yes."

I was amazed as I turned the pages. The book was filled with difficult sums. There was very little in the child's handwriting. I asked again, "Who has done these sums?"

Baby said, "My teacher, he always did sums in my book."

It was true. I could not understand why those difficult mathematical problems were worked out in a little child's exercise book.

While turning the pages, I noticed that a part of a page was torn. When I observed closely, I found that something had been written on it and then torn. Because in the next page the impression of what had been written on top was still there. I tried to read the impression, but could not.

Baby was getting restless, "Why are you not drawing pictures for me?"

Suddenly I remembered a trick which was very popular when we were in school.

I asked Baby, "Do you want to see magic?"

Baby was very excited, "Yes, yes!"

I tore a small piece of paper and blackened it with the pencil. Then I rubbed it on the impression — just as the negatives of photographs become clear after being washed in chemicals, so too, some of the words on the impression became clearer.

"Om, Hring, Kling."

"New moon phase starts at eleven... five ..."

The words were illegible and incomplete. The first seemed to be some kind of *mantra*. But the handwriting surely belonged to Harinath.

Baby was not at all satisfied when she saw this magic. So I had to satisfy her by drawing pictures of different kinds of animals. I tore the paper with the unintelligible writings, and kept it with me.

Himangshu returned at about three thirty. The car returned silently and entered the garage at the back of the house. After some time I heard Himangshu's voice asking the bearer to serve tea.

Byomkesh returned in the evening. Kumar did not get down from the car as he was feeling feverish. We had another round of tea with Byomkesh. Dewanji also joined us. He asked Byomkesh, "What happened?"

Byomkesh sipped his tea and said, "Not much. Police think that Harinath is being sheltered in their houses by some tenants."

Dewanji said, "You don't think so?"

Byomkesh answered, "No, I think otherwise."

"You think Harinath is not alive."

Byomkesh was surprised, "How did you know? Oh, Ajit must have told you. Yes, that's what I think, but I may be wrong."

No one said anything for some time. I felt very uneasy. Byomkesh did not seem annoyed with me, but one can never make out his feelings from his face. Maybe he would take me to task when we are alone.

Kaligati said suddenly, "I think you are wrong — Harinath is alive."

Byomkesh looked at him and said, "Did you get to know anything?"

Kaligati said, "Not exactly, but I am sure he is hiding in that forest."

Byomkesh said startled, "In this cold? In the forest?"

"Yes, there is a little hut in the forest called the sadhu's hut — he hides there at night to save himself from wild animals."

Byomkesh asked, "Did you got any positive proof?"

"No, but I am nearly sure he is there."

Byomkesh said nothing.

While getting ready for bed, Byomkesh asked me, "Have you announced about our discovery of the quicksand to the world also?"

"No, no — about Harinath I just mentioned that..."

"Yes, yes," he sat on a chair.

I said defensively. "You didn't tell me not to tell anyone about your suspicion about Harinath not being alive..."

"So you regarded it as your solemn duty to broadcast it to the world. Anyway, what did you do this afternoon?"

I was relieved to find that he was not so angry. I told him all that had happened in the afternoon. I showed him that piece of paper which I tore from Baby's exercise book. Byomkesh looked at the paper, but did not show much interest.

"I know all this — I can even complete the second line in this paper — The new moon phase will begin at 11.45 p.m. Even Harinath had seen the almanac."

Byomkesh only smiled when he heard about Himangshu's furtive activities in the afternoon — I said, "I think he is trying to hide something from us. I feel he wasn't very happy to have us as guests either."

Byomkesh thumped my back and said, "You are quite right. You can't imagine what a perfect gentleman he is. He is really incomparable. That's why we should solve this case."

I was astounded. Byomkesh continued saying, "Anadi Sarkar has a daughter called Radha. I saw her today."

I looked at Byomkesh foolishly. Byomkesh said, "She is a pretty girl of twenty, but a widow We punish people if they give in to the vagaries of youth — some times the punishment is too severe — especially in the case of women. We don't consider that fact that human beings are susceptible to temptations — but we pass a judgement. Even a court of law has a thing called 'grave and sudden provocation' — but society makes no excuses for a sinner. But the person who finds a chink in the stone wall of harsh rules of the society to show — is really a great man."

I had never heard Byomkesh giving a lecture on the laws of the society — how Anadi Sarkar's daughter had unplugged his fountain of emotions was indeed a mystery to me; I stared at him in surprise.

Byomkesh was quiet for some time and then heaved a great sigh, "Another strange thing which I have noticed is that in these cases, women are the bitterest enemies of their own sex."

Neither of us spoke for some time. Byomkesh then said, "It's late. Let us go to sleep. I can't understand how this case will end. I have understood everything, but it is difficult to catch the culprit. We must set a trap, Ajit, do you understand — we must set a trap."

I was irritated, "If you want to say something, please speak clearly — or don't speak at all!"

"You didn't understand anything?"

"No."

"Strange, whatever doubts I had, vanished after I went to the town today. I can see it as clearly as a film."

"So, what did you do in the town?"

Byomkesh said, "Only two things — I saw Anadi Sarkar's daughter at the station — I was hiding there for that. Then I got some documents in the Registry Office."

"Were you so late because of that?"

"Yes, it took a lot of time to have a look at the documents in the office — many permissions had to be taken."

"Then?"

"Then we came back." Byomkesh slipped inside his quilt. I knew that he was not going to tell me anything more. Very annoyed, I too tried to go to sleep.

As I was dozing off, we heard a soft knock on our door. Byomkesh opened the door, and to our surprise we found Kaligati standing at our door, wrapped in a black blanket. He said, "Come with me, I want to show you something. Ajitbabu, you also come along with us."

Byomkesh wore his coat and I wrapped a heavy shawl around myself and followed him. We went out of the house towards the gate and then into Kaligati's house.

There did not seem to be anyone in the house, we climbed onto the terrace by a staircase connecting the ground floor with the first floor. He took us to one side of the terrace and pointed towards the direction of the forest, "Can you see anything?"

We looked through the darkness of the night and noticed a light burning far away.

Byomkesh said, "A light is burning — could be a fire also. Where is it burning?"

Kaligati said, "It is burning in the hut in the forest."

"Oh, the hut in which the sadhu stayed? Has he come back?" Byomkesh mocked.

"No, I think it is Harinath."

"Oh!" Byomkesh seemed startled, "Yes, you did mention it this evening. But what is he doing there?"

"Probably he is unable to bear the cold — so he has lit a fire."

"Maybe ... maybe," Byomkesh said after much thought, "If he is alive — it is possible that he is there."

Kaligati said, "Byomkesh, he is alive. He is hiding from the police. Who will go into that hut at this time of the night but him?"

"That's true,' Byomkesh seemed thoughtful, then he said, 'Whoever it is we must find out. Ajit, are you ready to go there?"

I shivered, "Now?"

Kaligati said, "Please consider everything carefully. If you can catch him, then you must go now. It is very dark, but you cannot go with a light — he will run away if he sees a light. Again... it is impossible to reach there without making a noise. Think well before you decide anything."

We talked about what to do. Then we decided that it was not safe to go there that night because if he became suspicious, he would never come to that hut again.

Byomkesh said, "Dewanji is correct. We should not go tonight. I have a plan. If the culprit is not alerted — he will come there again tomorrow. Tomorrow Ajit and I will go and hide in that hut. Then as soon as he comes...."

Kaligati said, "That's not a bad plan. We will think about it. This much for today."

We came back to our own room. Dewanji saw us to our room. He asked Byomkesh, "You don't believe in sadhus?'

Byomkesh said vehemently, "I think they are all licentious cheats — that's my experience."

Kaligati's eyes dimmed with unexpressed anger. He gave a faint, forced smile and said, "All right, go to bed. Don't tell Himangshu about all this now."

Byomkesh said, "Yes, it is best not to tell him anything now."

Kaligati left the room. We again went to bed. Byomkesh said, "The old Brahmin is furious with me."

I said, "Yes, the way he glared at you before leaving — I think so too. Why did you have to say anything against sadhus when you know his belief in them?"

Byomkesh said, "I badly want him to be angry with me."

I could not understand what he meant by that. It was unlike Byomkesh to speak against someone's religious belief — but why did he do this today? I said, "What do you mean? What was the point in hurting the old man?"

"You will understand tomorrow, go to sleep now," he turned on his side.

Byomkesh whiled away his time till noon the next day, Himangshu seemed happy and relieved for some reason. He chatted and entertained us with many stories about his hunting experiences. He seemed to have forgotten that we were his guests to solve some serious mystery — he did not bring up that topic even once.

After our afternoon tea, Byomkesh took Kaligati aside and whispered to him, "We will proceed according to last night's plan — all right?"

Kaligati looked worried, "Have you given it a serious thought?"

Byomkesh said, "I think we should go to the hut tonight. We have to solve this mystery once and for all. The moon will set at about ten at night. Ajit and I will go there before that and wait for the culprit to come, and catch him as soon as he walks in!"

Kaligati said, "But if he does not come?"

Byomkesh said, "Then I'll assume that my earlier guess was correct — Harinath is dead."

Kaligati thought for some time and said, "But I think you should go once before to the hut now to see where it is — let's go!"

Byomkesh said, "All right, if we don't see it in daylight, it will be difficult for us to locate it in the dark." He did not reveal to Kaligati that we had already seen the hut. The three of us reached the hut. Kaligati walked ahead, and took us inside. We saw that there was a heap of ashes in the middle of the room — otherwise there was no change.

Kaligati opened the back door overlooking the stretch of sand. Byomkesh said, "What a lovely open space!"

I repeated, "Yes, yes!"

Kaligati said, "You will stay in this room tonight.... but I am a little nervous about it. I have heard people say that a tiger has come to the forest."

I said, "So what, — we will bring our guns!"

Kaligati smiled, "It will be so dark that you will not be able to see your target. Your guns will be of no use. Anyway, I hope the rumour about the tiger is false. There is no need to bring a gun. But we can't be too careful — so please be on the alert. In case you hear the roar of a tiger — don't stay inside this room. Come out of this back door, close it, go down on to the sandy area, and stand there. Even if the tiger enters the hut, it will not be able to climb down on to the sand."

Byomkesh said happily, "That's a good idea. We should not bother to bring guns. Besides Ajit has newly learnt to use a gun — he will needlessly make a noise, and all our efforts will go to waste."

We returned home. But my mind was covered by a mist. In the evening, we were sitting together in Himangshu's armoury, when Byomkesh asked, "Himangshubabu, suppose that a person had killed a simple, harmless, dependent man for his own selfish ends. How should that man be punished?"

Himangshu said with a smile, "Death — a tooth for a tooth, an eye for an eye."

Byomkesh turned to me, "Ajit, what is your opinion?"

"I agree with Himangshubabu."

Byomkesh was silent for some time. Then he went to the door and shut it. He came back and said softly, 'Tonight Ajit and I are going to hide in the small hut near the forest.'

Surprised, Himangshu said, "But why?"

Byomkesh gave him the reason in brief and said, "But we are feeling nervous to go alone. You have to come along with us."

Himangshu said with great enthusiasm, "Of course, I will come with you."

Byomkesh said, "But not a soul must know that you are coming. Then all our plans will go haywire. Listen, we will go out at about nine thirty in the night. You will start out of the house at ten — but no one must know. You must not let any one know that you are even aware of our plans. That is also important for the success of our expedition. And you must take your best rifle with you. We will go without any arms."

We got ready to go after the dinner, and left the house at exactly nine thirty.

As soon as we went out of the gate, we heard a voice calling us softly. It was Dewan Kaligati. He was waiting for us. He came near us and said, "Are you going now? I can see that you have not taken any guns with you. Remember what you must do if you should hear the roar of a tiger — go and stand on the stretch of sand behind the hut."

"Yes, we will remember your instructions."

"Good luck — may God be with you."

We began walking. Once we reached the hut, Byomkesh took out his torch and looked around the room. Then he sat on the ground, and told me to do the same. I sat down and asked, "May I light a cigarette?"

"Yes, but the light of the matchstick must not be seen from outside."

So we sat smoking silently. We heard a noise outside after half an hour. Byomkesh said, "Himangshubabu, come in."

Himangshu came in with a rifle. The three of us began our long vigil inside the hut.

At about 12.25 a.m. we heard a terrible sound very close by. All the three of us stood up. I had not heard the roar of a hungry wild tiger before — so I trembled with fear. Himangshu said in an undertone, "Tiger!" A slight sound from his direction told us that he was getting ready.

The roar had come from the side of the forest — so Himangshu quietly went to the doorless side of the hut. We stood motionless.

Himangshu whispered to us, "I can't see a thing; it is very dark."

Byomkesh whispered back, 'Shoot at the sound — you are an expert at it.'

Himangshu went a few steps out of the hut.

Just at that time, the earth trembled with a wild roar — it was very near us — maybe within fifty yards from where we stood. Before the echo of the roar receded, Himangshu fired from his rifle.

We heard the thud of something heavy falling at a distance. Himangshu said, "It has fallen, Byomkeshbabu, take out your torch!"

Byomkesh walked ahead of us with his torch. Himangshu said, "Don't go too near it — if it is only wounded — it will be dangerous!"

But where was the tiger! At the edge of the forest, something wrapped in a black blanket was lying on the ground.

Byomkesh shone the torch on it. Himangshu gave a shocked cry, "What is this? It's Dewanji!"

Dewan Kaligati was lying dead on the ground — his last expression revealing all the ugliness which he had so carefully hidden when he was alive.

Byomkesh examined him and said without a trace of remorse, "Dead. If there is something called the next world, then he must have met the man he had murdered — Harinath Choudhury — the tutor."

Byomkesh pushed the account books towards Himangshu, "If you examine these carefully, you will realise why you are running into debts of lakhs of rupees."

We were sitting in the drawing room. Two days had passed after the death of Kaligati. We had retrieved the stolen account books of the last four years by breaking open the cupboard in his house. Many other documents were also found there.

Himangshu had still not recovered fully from the trauma of the recent incidents. He sat quietly on one side. He said softly, "I still can't understand anything clearly."

Byomkesh said sympathetically, "That's understandable. I will unravel the mystery of this story from the bits and pieces of evidence which I have collected over the past few days. But before that, take these registered deeds."

"What are these?" said a bewildered Himangshu. Byomkesh said, "These are the registered papers of the deeds of mortgage which you had given to the moneylender to borrow money. The moneylender sold these deeds to Kaligati, who bought them with your money in his own name. These are the registered papers for those, and here are the receipts of the money which the money lender received from Kaligati. All the land you were mortgaging was becoming Kaligati's own in this way. He was buying your land with money stolen from you."

Himangshu shook his head helplessly.

"Kaligati was going to buy your whole estate from you at the end — that was his plan. He would have done it in about two years.... But the Maths-crazy tutor spoiled everything for him."

I said, "Please start at the very beginning."

Byomkesh said, "After Himangshubabu's father died, Kaligati saw that the new zaminder was quite disinterested in the running of the estate. He got a golden opportunity. He was the one who wrote the account books — there was no one else who checked them. So he started embezzling money with impunity. This went on for some time. His greed began to increase. But, then, there was a limit to the income and expenditure of an estate. So his theft was becoming limited. Now he began court cases with some of the rich tenants. The expense incurred in these was unlimited — this helped to make his theft unlimited too. He became ambitious — he began to dream of becoming the zaminder of Chorabali Estate. But you were not aware of anything.

"Things were going his way, when suddenly Harinath appeared on the scene. He was a simple person who had great respect for you. Kaligati began to initiate him into the worship of goddess Kali.

"But the problem was that he was not satisfied only with religion. He was crazy about Maths. He worked out huge mathematical problems in Baby's exercise books.

"One day his eyes fell on the huge account books in the cupboards of his room. He began examining the accounts, and was amazed at the discrepancies there. He was disturbed, but who was he going to talk to about all this?

He hardly used to meet you, and he was a bit frightened of you too. So he did the most normal thing — he confided in Kaligati about all the lapses in the account books.

"Kaligati was very worried. He decided that Harinath had to be removed, and also the four most recent account books of the last four years.

"Now begins the most terrible and cruel part of my story. Harinath had to die, but one could not use weapons against him. So what was Kaligati to do?

"Kaligati knew the area of the quicksand. Most probably, he too had discovered it as accidentally as we did, because he used to frequent the hut where his Guru, the sadhu, had been living for some months. This quicksand was just behind the hut.

"Kaligati thought out a novel way to get rid of the tutor. He would die, but no one would even know that he was dead! Kaligati would also be able to give a plausible excuse for the disappearance of the account books, while he himself would be beyond suspicion.

"On the last new moon night he told Harinath that if he wanted to attain the ultimate spiritual goal, he would have to go to the hut at midnight and chant prayers to goddess Kali. The tutor wrote the prayer down on Baby's exercise book, and kept the page with him.

"When everyone was asleep, Harinath went out of his room. He was going for prayers, so there was no need for him to take his shoes or wear his kurta, in fact it was so dark that he had to virtually feel his way to the hut — so there was no need to take his spectacles either. Besides, Kaligati must have taken him to the hut. Before coming away he told

Harinath, 'If you hear the roar of the tiger — go down by the back door of the hut and stand on the stretch of sand.'

"Harinath started praying, soon he heard the roar of the tiger — so authentic that even a veteran hunter like Himangshubabu could not make out the difference. This roar must have been heard by the villagers — so there was a rumour that a tiger was around. Kaligati was a talented person — he could imitiate the calls of animals so well that no one could make out the difference. We had heard him imitating a fox for Baby.

"Hearing a tiger roar, poor Harinath ran down, and stood on the stretch of sand, only to be sucked in by the quicksand! A shiver runs down one's spine when one thinks of his terrible helpless death!"

Byomkesh continued after a silence, "Now Kaligati returned home, removed the account books, and put them in his own cupboard in his house. The next day he proclaimed that Harinath had run away with the account books at the behest of some troublesome tenants.

"Still, to leave no doubt in anyone's mind, he even stole six thousand rupees, borrowed from the moneylender to cover the cost of court cases. Himangshu was always careless with his keys, and misplaced them — so this gave a golden opportunity to Kaligati to say that Harinath had stolen the keys of the locker. Then Ajit and I came on the scene. At this time something else was happening in the house which had no connection with Harinath's disappearance. It was an eternal tragedy of our critical society — a widow falling into the trap of temptation ... Anadi Sarkar's widowed daughter Radha had given birth to a still-born baby. This came to the ears of Himangshubabu's wife, who thought that Radha had committed the sin of killing a foetus. She came and told Himangshubabu that this could not be allowed or pardoned in her house — they must be thrown out. Isn't it so, Himangshubabu?"

Surprised, Himangshu nodded his head.

"But a kind person like you was reluctant to do that. You even had an argument with your wife. Then quietly you put the girl in a train and sent her to her aunt in Benares. You drove her to the station yourself to avoid gossip. You even offered to help her out with money. Anadi Sarkar is lucky to have such a generous master in you.

"This incident got so entangled with the incident of Harinath's disappearance, that at one time the whole thing became very complicated. It took me some time to unwind the whole mess. I hid in the station to see Radha, and realised that she had nothing to do with this mystery. I knew then that Kaligati was the murderer. I got a burning proof of the wickedness of the unscrupulous villain when I went through the documents in the Registry Office. There was no way in which I could catch him although I was sure of his crime.

"Kaligati was not worried in the beginning. But when he heard from Ajit that I had suspected that Harinath was dead — he became uneasy. He first tried to convince me that Harinath was alive, and took us to his terrace to show the fire in the hut, which he himself had lighted. I began to pretend that he could be correct and expressed a wish to catch the culprit red-handed by lying in wait for him in the hut. I was laying a trap for Kaligati but he thought that he was laying a trap for us. He knew that if Harinath did not come to the hut — which Kaligati knew more than anyone else that he would not — I would again start my investigations. So he decided to send us to the same fate as Harinath's. I, too, was waiting for this chance. He was a fanatic — he hated my jeering words about sadhus and his determination to kill me grew stronger in his mind. He took us to the hut that evening and gave us the same advice which he had given Harinath. The rest you know."

No one spoke for some time. Then Himangshu said, "Why did you ask me to go to the hut with my rifle? You knew I would aim at the unseen tiger just by hearing the roar."

Byomkesh smiled slightly, "Don't ask me that question. Don't he upset. Death was his only punishment. Instead of hanging in the gallows, he died in your hands — he is lucky, remember, you had said that night — an eye for an eye, a tooth for a tooth — you were only an instrument to mete out justice."

A car stopped at the porch of the house. Kumar Tridib got down with an anxious face and a newspaper in his hand. He entered the room and said, "What's all this? Kaligati was shot dead? I was down with influenza, so I could not come here the last few days. I saw this in the papers, and came rushing. Byomkesh, what has happened?"

Byomkesh read aloud the news item in the paper:

"The zaminder of Chorabali Estate in North Bengal had gone out to hunt with a few friends. He fired after hearing the roars of a tiger. But unfortunately the shot hit his old dewan Kaligati Bhattacharjee. It is anyone's guess what the old dewan was doing in the forest so late at night. Himangshubabu, the zaminder, is heartbroken at this accident. The police have completely exonerated Himangshubabu as the investigation showed that he had taken ample care and was totally in his senses when this accident occurred."

Byomkesh got up and told Kumar, "Let's go back to your estate now. We have finished the work here. I will relate to you the story of the sad demise of Kaligati while driving to your house."

Room Number Two
(Room Number Two)

The manager of Nirupama Hotel, Harishchandra Hore, looked at his watch — six thirty! He quickly sat up in bed. It was very late today. He called, "Gunadhar!"

The uniformed bearer appeared at his door. He was a thin man, very alert and efficient. Harish asked him, "Have you given the guests their bed-tea?"

Gunadhar said, "Yes. Everyone in the second floor has taken bed-tea, but Room Number Two of the first floor did not respond even when I knocked."

Harishchandra said, "Room number two of the first floor? ... Rajkumarbabu. Knock again after fifteen minutes.... Who has gone to the market?"

"Sarkar, Sir, has gone with General."

"All right, please bring me my tea." Harishchandra went into the adjoining bathroom.

Nirupama Hotel was situated on Rashbehari Avenue, a little further away from the Gariahat Square. The hotel was a little westernised. The servants wore smart uniforms. A doorman, also smartly dressed like a General, would stand at the gateway, and salute the right people.

It was a three storeyed house, and each storey had eight rooms. The manager occupied two rooms in the ground floor — one was his bedroom, the other, his office. On the ground floor was a large dining hall, furnished with tables and chairs, together with kitchen, servants' quarters, store-room etc. Both Indian and western dishes were available there. The charges were quite high. No wonder the hotel was frequented by upper-middle class guests.

Half an hour later, Harishchandra came out of his room, smartly dressed in a suit. He was a good-looking man of about forty-six, very alert and intelligent.

He had his breakfast in the dining room. His breakfast over, Harishchandra asked Gunadhar, "Did you go to Rajkumarbabu's room again?"

Gunadhar said, "Yes, … but this time too, he did not respond."

Harishchandra frowned. Then he went to his office. He took out his bunch of keys from the cupboard, came back, and said, "Let's go."

It was about seven in the morning. There was a great deal of hustle and bustle in the kitchen and the dining room. At eight, breakfast would have to be served to the guests.

While climbing the steps, Harishchandra asked Gunadhar, "Was Rajkumarbabu in his room last night?"

Gunadhar said, "Yes Sir, he was. I myself served him dinner in his room last night."

"When was the main door closed?"

"You came back at eleven last night, and then I shut the door."

By that time they had reached the first floor. There were eight rooms in a row on the first floor, and in front of these was a long verandah. All the doors were closed. Harishchandra stood in front of Room Number 2 and knocked peremptorily.

No one responded. He called out. "Rajkumarbabu!"

Still there was no response. Harishchandra tried the door, but the door did not open. This time Harishchandra raised his voice and called out loudly, "Rajkumarbabu!" The echo of his voice slowly gave way to an empty silence.

Harishchandra took out the duplicate key from his bunch. By now the doors on either side of Room Number Two had opened. Two heads were sticking out of them. An elderly lady from Room Number One asked, "What's the matter?" A middle-aged man from Room Number Three said, "Manager, please call a doctor.... I am running a temperature."

The lady came out of her room. "I am a doctor." She walked past Harishchandra and went to Room Number Three. The boarder, Shachitosh Sanyal, looked at her with bloodshot eyes, stood aside and said, "Please come in."

In the meantime, Harishchandra had opened the lock with his keys, pushed open the door a little. ... and stood stock still; then he quickly pulled the door shut.

There was no one on the verandah. He looked this side and that, lowered his voice and said, "Gunadhar, stay here, don't move ... I'll come back right now." His voice was full of fear and excitement.

He tiptoed downstairs ... In Room Number Three, the lady doctor asked Mr. Sanyal to lie down, took his temperature, felt his pulse, then said, "Nothing much, you must have caught a cold. Have two aspirins and go to bed.'

Shachitosh said, 'Is the fever very high?"

"No, only ninety-nine degrees."

"But my whole body is aching."

"That's nothing. This often happens during the change of season. I am sending you the aspirin tablets."

"What are your fees?"

"You don't have to pay me."

She came out of Room Number Three, and found Gunadhar waiting in front of Room Number Two. She asked, "What has happened in this room?"

Gunadhar shook his head, indicating that he did not know. Dr. Shobhona Roy did not ask any more questions, but entered her own room.

Harishchandra in the meantime was ringing up the police from the office room, "Please come fast, ... there has been a murder in my hotel!"

Byomkesh Bakshi, the Truth Seeker, had been invited the previous night to dinner in the house of the police inspector, Rakhal Sarkar. The latter was in charge of a police station in the southern part of Calcutta. Byomkesh had met Sarkar in connection with various cases. Sarkar was an amiable and friendly man. Although he was much younger than Byomkesh, they had become good friends. Sarkar, in fact, was very respectful towards him too.

It was quite late by the time dinner was over. Rakhal began repeatedly to request Byomkesh to spend the night with him. Finally, Byomkesh agreed. The two chatted late into the night.

The next day Byomkesh was getting ready to return home at quarter to eight, after breakfast, when the telephone rang. Rakhal picked up the phone and listened attentively for some time, then spoke a few words and kept the phone down. He turned to Byomkesh and said, "It was a phone from my police station. There has been a murder in a hotel in my area. It seems a mysterious affair — do you want to come with me?"

Byomkesh said, "Mysterious death? Of course I will come!"

When Rakhal Sarkar arrived at Nirupama Hotel with Byomkesh, a sub-inspector had already reached there with a few constables. One of them was standing at the doorway. No one was being allowed to leave or come into the hotel.

Rakhal entered Harishchandra's office and found the police doctor with his customary black bag, waiting there. Rakhal greeted the doctor; then turning to Harishchandra he said, "Are you the manager of this hotel?"

"Yes, Sir."

"And, you discovered the dead body?"

"Yes."

Inspector Sarkar and Byomkesh sat down on two chairs. The former said, "Tell us briefly whatever you know."

Harishchandra repeated everything that had happened that morning. Rakhal, Byomkesh and the doctor got up to examine the room and the dead body. Harishchandra went ahead to show the way.

Instead of Gunadhar, a constable was standing in front of Room Number Two now. Harishchandra opened the door with his keys.

Inside the room, a man — wearing a lungi and vest — was lying on the floor, on his right side, right in front of the door. It was startling to see his face. It seemed as if his face had been cut in strips and then stitched together very badly. But neither the cuts, nor the stitches, were very recent. The old wounds made his face look ugly.

The cause of the death, though, was quite different. There was some clotted blood on his vest. Rakhal Sarkar observed the body from outside the door, then turned to the doctor, "Doctor, please examine the body. After you finish your work, we'll go inside."

The doctor went in, while the rest of them stood outside. Byomkesh looked unobtrusively at the manager — on whose face there was still an expression of sheer fear.

"What is this? I have to go out just now, but the police is not allowing us even to step out of this place! What's the meaning of all this?" The trio turned round when they heard the irritated voice of a lady behind them.

Rakhal asked the angry lady, "But, who are you?"

Harishchandra explained, "She is staying in Room Number One, Dr. Mrs. Shobhona Roy."

Rakhal said politely, "A gentleman has been murdered in this room. So we cannot allow any boarder to leave without being questioned. But I promise you that I will take your testimony first of all, and let you go."

The lady looked frightened, "Murder, in the room next to mine! Who? When?"

Rakhal said, "We don't know anything as yet. Please go and wait in your room. We are coming just now."

The lady hesitated, tried to peep into Room Number Two, then went back to her room.

Two sub-inspectors had arrived in the meantime. Rakhal told them, 'One of you go to the second floor and the other to the first, ... and get the names and addresses of all the guests. Find out where each one was last night. Don't go to Room Number One and Three, I will question the boarders in these two rooms.'

The sub-inspectors went off. The doctor came out of Room Number Two after about five minutes, and said, "Now you can remove the body."

Rakhal said, "What did you see?"

The doctor said, "He was killed with a knife, either with a knife ... or something sharp like that. It pierced the ribs and went right into the heart. It is the work of a professional murderer. There was no other wound except that one; the weapon pierced the right spot in one attempt."

"Time of death?"

"Can't say anything for certain without an autopsy. Most probably between nine o'clock last night to twelve mid-night."

Byomkesh said, "How old are the scars on his face?'

"Ten to twelve years old."

"How old was Rajkumar himself?"

"Ah ... around forty years, to my mind ... Well, I am leaving now; send the body. I'll send you the report tomorrow after the post-mortem." The doctor left.

Rakhal Sarkar said to Harishchandra, "Go and do your work now. Give me the key to this room. Be in the office please."

About half an hour later, after transferring the body, Rakhal looked at Byomkesh and asked, "What next?"

Byomkesh pointed to Room Number One, "You better finish questioning the lady. She is a woman and a doctor. So she gets the first preferences."

"All right. After we finish with her, we will have a good look in this room." He locked the door of Room Number Two, and then knocked at Room Number One. The door opened at once. The lady looked displaced. She was stout and short — but her body seemed to be bursting with impatience.

She said, "Please let me go quickly. Inspector, my work is suffering."

"I'll let you go, Madam, after asking you just a few absolutely necessary questions!" Rakhal started writing in his notebook, even as he spoke.

"Your full name?"

"Mrs. Shobhona Roy."

"Age?"

"Forty-nine,"

"Husband's name?"

"Late Ramratan Roy."

"Where do you practice?"

"In Beharampur."

"Why have you come to Calcutta?"

"I am a gynaecologist — I have a contract with the Seva Sadan — so I have to come to Calcutta some times."

"Do you not have any relatives in Calcutta?"

"I have no one anywhere."

"Children?"

"I had a daughter. She died many years back." Her face hardened for a minute, then became normal again. She was not beautiful — but with that harsh expression — she looked positively ugly for a while.

"Do you stay here when you come to Calcutta?"

"Yes. This hotel is convenient for me."

"When did you come this time?"

"Day before yesterday."

"Last night, a man called Rajkumar Basu was murdered in the next room. Did you know him?"

"No, I have never heard of him."

"Did you never meet him before? Your rooms were next to each other, hence the question."

"No, I would have remembered a face like that."

"Where were you at eight thirty in the evening yesterday?"

"I came back after eight from the Seva Sadan; then I washed, changed and went down to have dinner in the dining room below. I came to my room again before nine, after my dinner — and did not go out again."

"Did you hear anything at night?"

"I got into bed at about quarter part nine — but I could not sleep properly for the disturbance in the next room."

"Was there any noise in the next room?"

"No — but the door was continuously opening and closing — that was disturbing me."

"What time was it?"

"I did not see the watch — must have been between half past nine and ten."

"Did you do anything about it?"

"What could I do? Many inconsiderate people come to the hotel — they don't bother about others."

"When did you get to know about the murder?"

"I knew about the murder from you. After bed-tea, I was ready to go down for breakfast, when I heard knocking and pushing next door. I came out of my room and found the manager. When I asked him what was wrong, he did not say anything. Then I went to Room Number Three."

"Why?"

"The gentleman there was unwell, and looking for a doctor. So I went to see him."

"Did you know him earlier?"

"I had seen him earlier, but I did not know him. I don't even know his name."

"What was wrong with him?"

"He had just caught a cold — nothing much."

There was nothing more to ask. Inspector Rakhal Sarkar said, "You may leave for your work. But, please, don't leave Calcutta without letting the police know."

Shobhona Roy looked very irritated. She did not reply, but got up with the bag in her hand.

While opening the door of Room Number Two, Rakhal said, "She is a bit ill-tempered. She was not frightened at all. Probably she is used to the police — after all she is a doctor. Now let's see if the murderer has left any clue.... Constable Hajra, go down to the office below and ring the head office to send finger-print experts at once."

Rakhal and Byomkesh went into the room, and shut the door from inside.

The room was ten feet by twelve feet. There was a bed, a small table and chair, a mirror hung from the wall, next to it was a rack for clothes; a fan was hanging from the ceiling. Both the men looked round the room.

Rakhal said, "Have you seen the bed?"

"Yes — both the bed and the rack."

"From the bed it was obvious that Rajkumar Basu had slept there, after changing into a lungi and vest from a dhoti and kurta. There had been a knock on the door. When he opened the door, the murderer stabbed him with a knife. He fell, and did not get up again. The murderer pulled the door shut from outside, and left. I feel the murderer did not even enter the room. So the finger-print expert will find no finger-prints other than Rajkumar's. The murderer's finger-prints could have been found on the handle of the door, perhaps, but by now it would have got rubbed off since so many people had touched it."

Rakhal said, "That's true; but still, let us search the room."

Byomkesh said, 'You do it — I don't want to touch any thing — the finger-print experts will be more confused then.'

Rakhal started his job systematically. He began with the drawers of the table, pockets of the kurta, then he looked under the mattress. He searched everywhere, but got nothing. Then he pulled out a suitcase from under the bed. This was the only luggage of the dead man in the room.

The suitcase was unlocked. Rakhal opened the lid. There were two sets of clothes in the suitcase. Beneath the clothes were a bundle of ten rupee notes, and a small diary.

Rakhal counted the notes, which amounted to rupees twelve hundred.

He said, "The person who had murdered him was not interested in money." On the first page of the diary was written — Sukanto Som. Rakhal showed it to Byomkesh who replied. "So Rajkumar is a false name. But Sukanto Som — the name rings a bell ... have you heard?"

Rakhal said, "No, I can't remember having heard it ever." He began turning the pages of the diary. Every page had the name of a city or town written on top — for example — Varanasi, Calcutta, Cuttak. Below the names of towns and cities, were the names of some individuals with their addresses and phone numbers. On the page for Calcutta, there were four names and addresses — and next to them was a certain sum of money. For example:

Mohonlal Kundu 117 D, Panapukar Lane	Rs. 5000
Shyamakanta Lahiri 30/1, Lake Colony	Rs. 4000
Jagabandhu Patra 56, Ram Bhaduri Lane	Rs. 3000
Latika Choudhury 17, Gandhi Park	Rs. 4000

Rakhal said, "Can you make head or tail of these?"

Byomkesh examined the book and said, "I suspect that the profession of this man was blackmailing."

"Why? He could have been an insurance agent!"

"Maybe. But an insurance agent is not a target for murder nor do they move around with false names."

"So you feel that one of those whom Rajkumar was blackmailing, has murdered him?"

"We could question these people whose names are in his diary on the page marked for Calcutta. Then we may get some clue. Let us now meet the man in Room Number Three."

"Let's."

Shachitosh Sanyal was lying flat on his bed. Hearing footsteps, he lifted his head and asked, "Who is that?"

Rakhal said briefly, "Police."

Shachitosh sat up in bed with rounded eyes. "Police? What do you want?"

Rakhal said, "We want to ask you a few questions. I think you have heard that the boarder in Room Number Two has been murdered?"

Shachitosh was quiet for a moment, then he said, "Murdered? Who has been murdered?"

Room Number Three was similar in size and shape as the other two rooms. Rakhal sat on the bed, Byomkesh on a chair.

Rakhal said, "The gentleman who was staying in Room Number Two was murdered last night. His name was Rajkumar Basu. Did you know him?"

"Rajkumar Basu? No, I didn't know him. Who has murdered him?"

"We don't know that as yet... What is your name?"

"Shachitosh Sanyal."

"Where do you stay?"

"Bhagalpur. I am ill. The doctor has asked me to lie down."

"Which doctor?"

"The lady doctor. I have caught a cold, she has asked me to take aspirin tablets and lie down. Tell me, are women doctors good?"

"Maybe. How did you catch a cold?"

"I went out last evening without wearing warm garments — I think I caught a cold then."

"You did not go out at night?"

"No, I had my dinner at nine in the dining room, and then came back to my own room. I did not go out after that."

"When did you come to Calcutta?"

"Three days back — I was supposed to go back today, but..."

"Why have you come to Calcutta?"

"I do business in ghee — I am a regular supplier to Ganguram — the famous chain of sweet shops in Calcutta. So I have to come here some times. Tell me, do you think my cold will take a bad turn for pneumonia?"

"I don't think so — you look very healthy to me. How old are you?"

"Forty-two. Maybe I look healthy but I am actually very frail. I catch infections very fast. I am feeling very hungry. Tell me, if I eat anything will I feel worse?"

"Have some hot milk and bread.... So you did not know Rajkumar Basu?"

"No, I have never heard of him."

Byomkesh said, "Have you heard the name Sukanto?"

Shachitosh said, "Sukanto? No. The name of my brother-in-law is Srikantokumar Lahiri — he is dead."

Rakhal asked, "Did you hear any noise from the next room last night?"

"Noise? No. I lay in bed right after my dinner. My wife says that if I go to sleep even a band of robbers cannot wake me up. Was the man murdered with a gun?"

"No, with a knife." Rakhal stood up to leave, "Don't go out of Calcutta without informing the police. Let's go, Byomkesh."

Harishchandra was sitting in his office room; he asked Byomkesh and Rakhal in a nervous voice. "What happened?"

Rakhal did not answer his question, but said, "I will now take the testimony of the hotel staff. We will start with you. Sit down. What's your full name?"

"Harishchandra Hore."

"Do you stay here?"

"Yes."

"For how long have you been here?"

"Eight years now."

"What do you know about Rajkumar Basu?"

Harishchandra opened a thick log book.

"Rajkumar Basu's home address is Adampur, Patna, Bihar. For the last five years he has been coming here for two or three days, twice a year. He never went out of the hotel. He rang up a few friends from this office and they used to come and meet him in the late evenings. I don't know anything more than that."

"When did he come this time?"

"The day before yesterday."

"Did he ring up?"

"Yes, he rang up yesterday morning."

"Did Rajkumar always stay in Room No. 2?"

"No, he stayed in whichever room was vacant. But he took great care to see that he did not bump into any other person or boarder; probably he had a complex about his face."

"Did you know what profession he belonged to?"

"No, Sir."

"Were you in the hotel last night?"

"Sir...." he hesitated, "I went out for about two hours. I stay in the hotel, but my family lives in a rented accommodation, so I go and see them some times. Yesterday I went out after the guests had sat down for dinner. I came back at about eleven at night."

"Who takes charge of the hotel in your absence?"

"Gunadhar Das, the chief bearer."

"Please call him."

Gunadhar arrived.

"What do you know about Rajkumar Basu, the man who was murdered?"

"Sir, I don't know anything about him. He came here some times and stayed for two or three days — that's all."

"Did he not speak to you?"

"Very little, he asked me to do a few odd jobs, that's about all."

"Who looked after him?"

"I did, I gave him bed-tea in the morning, and brought all his meals to his room. I look after every guest on the first floor."

"So Rajkumar never went to the dining room."

"No, sir."

"When did you last see him yesterday?"

"I went into his room to serve his dinner at quarter to nine. Then I collected the empty dishes at about nine. He was very much alive then."

"Why do you think he never went to the dining room?"

"I don't know — probably because of his face — he did not like to come out when people were around."

"But people used to come to him?"

"Yes sir."

"Who visited him last night?"

"I don't know, General Singh will know."

'General Singh!'

"He is our gatekeeper. His name is Rampirit Singh, but everyone calls him General Singh."

"Call him."

The Bhojpuri gate keeper saluted them. He was tall and strongly built. He sported a huge moustache and wore a khaki uniform. Rakhal looked him up and down, "So you keep a watch at the gate of the hotel?"

"Yes sir, my duty is from nine to twelve in the morning and five to ten in the afternoon."

"Do you write down the names of the visitors who come to the hotel to meet the guests?"

"No sir, I have not been ordered to do that. I allow those who are decently dressed to go in after asking them whom they wish to meet."

"You don't stop anyone?"

"No, sir, if they are well-dressed — I don't."

"If they are not well-dressed, then?"

"Then I glare at them and ask them a hundred questions before I let them go."

"All right, now tell me, were there any visitors for Room No. 2 last night?"

"Yes, sir. Two gentlemen and one lady. They lady came at about 9:15 p.m. — asked me the room number of Rajkumar babu, went up the stairs. She went out of the hotel after about five or ten minutes."

"How old was she?"

"About twenty or twenty five — fair, slim and tall, she wore dark glasses."

"Then?"

"Then about 9:30 came a gentleman. He, too, took the number, went up and returned after five or ten minutes."

"Then?"

"At about a quarter to ten another man came. He was quite stout. He too went up and returned after five minutes. After that no one came during my duty hours."

Rakhal was happy with Rampirit General Singh's sharp memory. The gatekeeper saluted and left.

Byomkesh sat in the office with a frown. In the meantime the two sub-inspectors came down after questioning the other guests.

Rakhal asked, "What happened?"

One of them said, "I went to the second floor. I have written down their names and addresses. All are saying that they did not go out of their room after dinner."

"Are they telling the truth?"

"That is difficult to verify. But a servant sleeps at night on the landing of the second floor. It is difficult to climb over him and go down the steps. I asked the servant — he said that he had gone to sleep at ten thirty and no one went down after that."

"What about you?" Rakhal turned to the other sub-inspector.

"It is the same story. I have taken the names and addresses of all the guests on the first floor. Here another servant sleeps on the landing. He said that he had gone to sleep at about quarter to eleven and no one went down after that."

Rakhal asked the manager, "Why do you make the servants sleep on the landing?"

The manager said, "We have made this arrangement in case any guest needs anything at night."

It was twelve noon by then. Rakhal told Byomkesh, "Let us leave now. We will eat somewhere outside, and then go and meet the four people mentioned in Rajkumar's diary."

Harishchandra said, "Sir, why should you have lunch outside — we will be grateful if you have it in our hotel."

After a good lunch Byomkesh, Rakhal and the other policemen came out of the hotel. Rakhal told one of the sub-inspectors, "Dutta, you stay here. This is the key of Room Number Two. The finger-print experts will come anytime now. I am going out with Byomkesh and Ghose."

They came out on the street. Rakhal said, "Goodness knows if we will get anyone at home at this time. First let us meet Jagabandhu Patra — he is from Orissa, I think."

Byomkesh said, "Yes."

"Why are you quiet today, Byomkeshbabu?"

"I am watching and listening — the time hasn't come for talking yet."

Soon they reached the house of Mr. Patra. He stayed in the ground floor of a three storeyed house. The man who came out in response to the doorbell, was bent and thin, aged about forty. Rakhal said, "Are you Jagabandhu Patra?"

"Yes," he seemed a bit nervous at seeing policemen at his doorstep, "What do you want?"

"Rajkumar Basu has been murdered in Nirupama hotel."

Jagabandhu was genuinely surprised, "Rajkumar has been murdered?"

"Yes, we want to ask you a few questions."

"Please come in," Jagabandhu took them to a room and asked them to sit, "Sit down, I am coming in a minute."

He went to the next room. The sitting room was small. There were a few chairs and a table, a telephone and a cupboard. Byomkesh lit a cigarette and looked here and there — but nothing told him anything about the character of Jagabandhu. Five minutes went by, then ten — there was no sight of the man. Rakhal raised his voice and called him, "Jagabandhu!" There was no answer.

Byomkesh smiled, "I think Jagabandhu babu has left the house!" Rakhal said excitedly, "Left the house! Come let's go in."

It was found that the back door was wide open.

Rakhal came back and said, "The bird has flown."

Byomkesh in the meantime was going through some books in the cupboard. He said, "The man was a tout in the Race Course."

"But why did he run away?" said Rakhal.

"There must be some grave problem — he would not have run away if it was only a matter of racing."

Rakhal immediately rang up the police station and asked for more force. He told the sub inspector, "Ghose, you remain here, the others will be here just now. Search the place thoroughly. Take finger prints. Inform the Head Office — the man must be a seasoned criminal. We are going out on some business."

After coming out of the house Rakhal asked Byomkesh, "Do you think Jagabandhu is the culprit?"

Byomkesh said, "Can't say. He looked very surprised when he heard the news of Rajkumar's death — but it could have been a pretence."

They went to Mohanlal Kumar's house next and found that he had gone to Benares with his wife and no one knew when he would return.

Then they went to Shyamakanta Lahiri's house. But he was not at home either — he had gone to office — he worked in the Port Commissioner's office. He would not be back before evening. Rakhal heaved a sigh, "Now we have only Latika Choudhury to visit. Since she's a lady, she will probably be at home at this time of the day."

Mrs Choudhury lived in a small, neat, independent house with a small garden in front. As soon as they rang the bell a lady came out and said, "Mr Choudhury is not at home." Then her eyes fell on Rakhal's police uniform and she looked nervous. She fitted whatever description General Singh had given, except that she was older, about thirty or thirty two, but still slim and good-looking.

Rakhal asked, "Are you Latika Choudhury?"

The lady said almost in a whisper, "Yes, what do you want?"

Rakhal said, "I want to ask you a few questions. I am from the police department."

The lady asked us in with a frightened expression. The sitting room was tastefully arranged. There was a half-bust photograph of a gentleman. He looked stern and his glance seemed to be following everyone all over the room.

Byomkesh and Rakhal sat on the same sofa. Mrs Choudhury sat nervously at the edge of a chair and looked at them.

"What is your husband's name?"

"Tarakumar Choudhury."

"His profession?"

"Engineer.... railway engineer."

"Your children?"

"We are childless."

"You went to Nirupama hotel at 9-15 last night."

Mrs. Choudhury stared at them with wide, frightened eyes, "No, no, I went to see a film."

"The gateman of the hotel saw you, and will be able to identify you."

Mrs. Choudhury still insisted, "But I went to see a film — I can even show you the counterfoil."

"But you came out of the hall before the film was over, then you went to Nirupama Hotel and met Rajkumar Basu."

She shook her head and said in a frightened voice, "I don't know Rajkumar Basu. I have never heard of any such person."

Byomkesh shot his first question at her, "Did you know Sukanto Sam?"

Mrs. Choudhury covered her face and began weeping bitterly.

Byomkesh said gently, "We know that Rajkumar Basu and Sukanto Som is one and the same person. You had gone to give him money at about a quarter to nine. Now you tell us everything. There is nothing to be afraid of."

Mrs. Choudhury kept on sobbing for some time, then wiped her eyes and said in a broken voice, "I can't understand why you want to know all this, but I will tell you everything.... But please see to it that my husband does not get to know anything."

Byomkesh pointed to the photograph, "That's your husband — he seems strict — no, we won't let him know anything."

The substance of what Mrs. Choudhury told them shamefacedly, was this: About twelve or thirteen years ago when she was a young girl, she was a different person. She regarded herself to be very modern, and free from prejudices. Her father had a lot of money, and the discipline at home was slack. So Latika Choudhury spent her time in unbridled fun in picnics, films, parties and theatre.

At that time there was a filmstar called Sukanto Som. He was not only a very good actor, but also very modern. Latika Choudhury fell madly in love with him. It was not just an ordinary romance of a young girl with a filmstar — it was much more than that. They were physically and mentally involved with each other. She used to write torrid love letters to him whenever he was away for shootings. She was desperate to marry him. But one day she got to know that Sukanto had a wife. She was heart-broken. Her father probably guessed what was happening; so he quickly arranged her marriage.

Two years went by. Her husband was good, but strict. He would not tolerate the fact that his wife had a love affair before her marriage. Latika gradually realised what a gem of a person her husband was, and came to love and respect him deeply. Though they had no children, now they were very much in love with each other and were happy.

One day she saw a terrible news in the papers. Sukanto had throttled his wife to death. The case went to court. But the culprit was released because he had killed his wife in self-defence, when his wife attacked him with a knife and tore his face and parts of his body into shreds. All through the case, Latika was very nervous in case her name came up in the court in any way. But neither the culprit nor the witnesses took her name. She heaved a sigh of relief.

Then again two years went by.

Sukanto was naturally not able to go back to films with a face like that. He just seemed to have disappeared. Suddenly, one day, he met her with that terrible face of his, in her house, in the absence of her husband.

He said, "I need money. You have to give me at least three thousand rupees every six months — I know that it is not much for you. In case you don't, I will send all those love letters which you wrote to me, to your husband."

From that time, Latika had been giving Sukanto that amount every six months. She was always frightened that her husband would get to know her secret.

Last night she had gone to Nirupama Hotel, she had given the money to Sukanto even without stepping into

Room Number Two, and had come away quickly. She did not know anything else.

After she finished her story, Byomkesh and Rakhal stood up to leave. Byomkesh said, "We are leaving. But before we go we will give you good news — Sukanto Som neé Rajkumar Basu was murdered last night between 9-15 and 11 p.m."

After coming out Rakhal said, "We heard her story, but it has not thrown any light on the murder."

Byomkesh said, "We can't say that the whole day has been unsuccessful. We have heard the testimonies of so many people — one person among them has disclosed something, but I just can't remember who said it or what he or she had said."

"Can't you remember anything?"

"No, it has just sunk into my subconscious."

Rakhal looked at his watch. It was nearly three in the afternoon. He said, "I am going to the police station now. What about you?"

"I will return home. I will meet you in the morning tomorrow. But if you get to know anything in the meantime — do ring me up."

Byomkesh returned home at about five in the evening. He had a cup of tea, and then sat down and lit a cigarette.

At about half past six, he sat up with a jerk! He smiled to himself and whispered, "I have remembered!"

He got ready to go out. He went to the office of the newspaper 'Kalketu' and went through the files of the last ten years.

The next morning, Byomkesh rang up Rakhal — "Did you get any news?"

Rakhal said, "Nothing special. We didn't get any new information about the body after the post-mortem. He died about one and half hours after dinner. Finger-prints of both Rajkumar and Gunadhar were found in the room. We went again to Shyamakanta Lahiri's house, he denied going to Nirupama Hotel, that night. But General Singh has identified him. We have not arrested him, but I have appointed a spy to keep a watch on him."

"Then?"

"We got to know that Jagabandhu Patra's real name is Bhagaban Mohanti. He is a hardened criminal. He had killed a woman in Midnapore and had served a sentence of fourteen years in prison. Then he escaped from jail, and was working as a tout here with a false name."

"Anything else?"

"Latika Choudhury's husband returned home that night after eleven — but we could not find out where he was as yet."

"There is no need to know that."

"Really?"

"What about the hotel?"

"The guests are becoming very restless and impatient. I am thinking of letting them go this afternoon. Did you find out anything?"

"Yes. I am going to Nirupama Hotel just now. You also come there."

Byomkesh and Rakhal stood in front of Room Number One and looked at each other. Then they knocked gently on the door.

The door opened and Dr. Shobhona Roy glared at Rakhal — "Look here, Inspector, how long are you going to keep me here? Do you know that it is against law to keep a doctor like me confined like this?"

Rakhal said, "If you have any complaint against me, there is the court for that. But right now I have a few questions for you."

Both the men entered the room, and Byomkesh sat on a chair.

He said, "Dr. Roy, I want to tell you a story."

Shobhona Roy was furious, "Who are you? You have the nerve to joke with me?"

Rakhal said, "He is Byomkesh Bakshi, the famous Truth Seeker. You must have heard of him."

Byomkesh said, "I am not joking at all. Please sit down."

Dr. Roy sat at the edge of the bed, and said a little quietly, "Please tell me quickly what you have to... I am surely going back to Beharampur today!"

Byomkesh said, "We will see about that.... I read this story in the newspaper — I am narrating it to you briefly ... Sukanto Som was a film artist."

Mrs. Roy's body stiffened. She stared unblinkingly at Byomkesh.

Byomkesh said drily, "So you do know him. Naturally — you know him — he was your son-in-law. Sukanto had made quite a name for himself in films. You were then practising in Burdwan. You were a widow, and lived with your only daughter. Sukanto used to visit Burdwan. One day he lured your daughter to elope with him. He had tempted her out of the house by promising to make her a heroine in his films. You disliked Sukanto. So the two had to elope.

"After living together for a few months each got a taste of the other's nature. They were horribly ill-tempered. Sukanto was a man with a loose character too. Moreover, your daughter was furious with him for not giving her a heroine's role in any of his films.

"One day, their fight reached a climax — and your daughter attacked him with a knife, and cut the skin and flesh of his face into shreds. To save himself Sukanto throttled your daughter.

"He was arrested, but had to remain in the police hospital for three months. When he was taken from there to the court — even the judge was shocked to see the terrible condition of his face. There was no arrangement for plastic surgery in the police hospital, so the doctors stitched up his face as best as they could. But that was the end of his film career.

"The verdict was given. You gave witness against Sukanto — but try as you did — you could not get him hanged. He had no weapons in his hands — your daughter did. So he was released on grounds of self-defence."

Dr. Roy said angrily with hatred in her eyes. "Lies. He killed my daughter first, and then he cut his face to escape the punishment."

Byomkesh shook his head, "That's not possible — a man can't hurt himself like that. Besides, he was as actor — his face was very important to him. He would never have done that to himself. Anyway, he escaped from being convicted in a murder case, but his film life had come to an end. He did not know of any honest way to earn a living. He escaped from Calcutta and settled in Patna and started his business of blackmailing people. In the last ten years, he had collected many clients all over India. He was getting a regular flow of money. This became his profession — to find out secrets in the lives of people, and then to blackmail them. He was never a good man.

"When Sukanto came to Calcutta, he stayed in this hotel. In the meantime, you went off to Beharampur from Burdwan and settled there. You too came to Calcutta on your own business and stayed in this hotel. But till lately, you had never met. Sukanto, usually, kept to his room.

"This time, accidentally, you saw him. He was in the room just next to yours. But he did not see you — or he would have been careful. You hated him for what he had done to your daughter. You were determined that if you ever met him you would kill him. This nurtured desire got the better of you when you saw him this time. You were determined that he had to die... Your daughter probably inherited your violent and wild nature.

"That night you waited in your room after dinner. You knew how you were going to kill him. You kept waiting for the right moment.

"From a quarter past nine, people began coming to Sukanto. You kept waiting. At ten, people stopped coming to him. You came out with your weapon.

"Other guests had already gone to bed in their rooms. The servant who slept on the landing had not yet come.

This was your chance. You knocked at his door and — as soon as he opened it — you stabbed his heart... You are a doctor — so you did not have to hesitate to find out the position of his heart. Then you pulled his door shut, came to your own room, and got ready for bed. No one knew that you had any connection with Rajkumar Basu: In fact the police suspected the people who had visited him that night — especially as most of them had criminal records in the past.

"But you had made a small mistake. When the Inspector was questioning you — you said that you had never seen Rajkumar, but in the same breath you told him too that you would have never forgotten such a face if you had seen it before! So, when did you see the face? You did try to peep in once — but all the three of us were standing at the door, and you could not have seen the face of a prostrate body then. Had you not made that fatal slip of tongue, I would not have thought of going through the news records of the last ten years."

By the time Byomkesh stopped speaking, Dr. Roy was panting like the bellow of an ironsmith. She was burning with fury.

She said through her clenched teeth, "Lies, all lies — Sukanto killed my daughter — but I did not kill him. How will I kill him? Do I have a knife?"

Byomkesh pointed to her bag of surgical kit, "Your weapon is inside that."

"No! have a look!" — She opened the bag and pulled out a separated part of a pair of thin, sharp surgical scissors! She quickly tried to stab herself with it, but Rakhal proved to be faster than her, and snatched away her weapon. The constables caught hold of the doctor who was screaming like a mad woman, "Let me go! Let me die!"

Byomkesh heaved a sigh of relief, "Thank God! We've got the instrument with which the murder was committed, — otherwise the crime would have been difficult to prove in the court!"